Copyright © 2023 by Jennie Marts
All rights reserved.

No part of this book may be reproduced in any form or by any electronic or mechanical means, including information storage and retrieval systems, without written permission from the author, except for the use of brief quotations in a book review. This eBook is licensed for your personal enjoyment only. This eBook may not be re-sold or given away to other people.

AI RESTRICTION: The author expressly prohibits any entity from using this publication for purposes of training artificial intelligence (AI) technologies to generate text, including without limitation technologies that are capable of generating works in the same style or genre as this publication. The author reserves all rights to license uses of this work for generative AI training and development of machine learning language models.

This book is a work of fiction. Names, characters, places, and incidents are either a product of fiction or are used in a fictitious manner, including portrayal of historical figures and situations. Any resemblance to actual persons living or dead is entirely coincidental.

Cover Design & Interior Format:
The Killion Group, Inc.

LOVE AT FIRST

JENNIE MARTS

*This book is dedicated to
anyone who has ever felt like you are not enough and
for those who have been abandoned and left behind…
You are stronger than you think and
you are not alone.*

CHAPTER ONE

FORD LASSITER, AND his brothers, Dodge and Chevy, had heard every joke in the book about their names. But the sad truth of it was that their Mama had named each of them after the truck that their individual deadbeat dads had driven away from them in.

Their mother had eventually abandoned them, too. But she'd driven off in a beat-up Honda Accord, after dropping them at their grandparents' ranch, then conveniently forgot to ever come back to pick them up again. Now he, *and* his brothers all drove the trucks of their namesakes, mostly to be contrary, but probably also a little to spite their Mama.

Ford drove a 1984 Seventh Generation F-series pickup that had belonged to his grandfather. It had been his first truck, a gift from his grandparents when he'd turned sixteen. He'd had it repainted navy blue and had rebuilt the engine twice. And she still purred like a kitten as he drove under the bare-timber arched *Lassiter Ranch* sign and pulled out onto the highway.

He didn't have far to go. Not that *anywhere* in the small Colorado mountain town of Woodland Hills was far to go, but this trip was only taking him to the neighboring ranch.

Still can't believe someone actually bought this place, he thought as he turned down the driveway and eyed the old farm.

He remembered Frank and Ida Johnson—the older couple who'd lived there for as long as he could remember. They'd been not just neighbors, but friends of his grandparents. Ida had occasionally watched them after school, and he and his brothers had helped bring in their hay every summer. Ida made the best oatmeal butterscotch cookies he'd ever tasted.

The house had been deserted for the last several years, and it hurt his heart a little to see how much it had fallen into disrepair. As Frank and Ida had aged, so had the house, and Frank hadn't been able to keep up with all the repairs, like fixing the porch or covering the wood siding with fresh paint. Ford hadn't been here in a year or so, but as he parked in front of the house, he could still remember the way it had looked when he was younger, and the place brought back good memories.

The once-cheery yellow two-story Victorian farmhouse had faded to almost white, and the sagging front porch, with its rotted wood and multiple holes, looked like a strong gust of wind could blow the whole dang thing right off. Most of the windows were cracked or broken, a few replaced with plywood, and the gutters hung loose on one side and were completely missing on the other. The wood looked to be rotted clear through on the steps leading up to the porch, and one of the banisters had plum fallen off and lay in the dirt next to the steps.

It had once had the charm of a quaint gingerbread house, with elaborate decorative corbels under the corniced roofline, dormer windows, and one corner of the house extending out in a round turret that went all the way up to an attic room at the top.

The small front yard, once full of flower gardens, was overrun with weeds, and the previously bright white picket fence had faded to a dull gray and leaned precariously close to the ground. Thankfully, the barn still stood strong. It was newer than the house, and just needed a fresh coat of paint to return it to its former glory.

He felt sorry for the new owner. This place looked like a big old money pit now. But all those repairs meant cash in the bank to him. Fall harvest was just around the corner, and one of their combine implements had just broken. It was going to cost a few thousand dollars to purchase a new one, so Ford had been downright grateful when the local real estate agent had called and asked if he'd be interested in a side gig to help renovate this place. The new owner had bought it sight unseen, and they were looking to hire someone with construction experience to help with the repairs and to fix it up.

Ford and his brothers had been working on their grandparents' ranch since they were kids. Duke, their granddad, had taught them everything from how to rope a steer to how to wield a chainsaw. They'd even spent a summer helping to renovate the hunting cabin in the mountains behind the ranch, adding a bedroom, a bathroom, and updating the kitchen with running water and appliances. Ford enjoyed working with his hands and watching a project come together. That summer, he'd learned everything construction-related, from floor joists to roof trusses, from plumbing to electrical.

And this house looked like it would need them all.

Thinking about the hunting cabin brought up memories of the amazing night he'd spent there earlier that summer with a woman who'd acted like she cared about him then left him behind.

His brothers razzed him about being a grump and spending too much time reading, or hanging out with his dog or his horse, and their razzing probably had some merit. He *was* a bit of a grouch, but that weekend, the one he'd spent with Elizabeth Cole, had been the most fun he'd had in years. And not just the time they'd spent in her bed *and* in the bed of his pickup—although he'd spent many nights since reliving those times—it was more than that. She'd made him laugh, and he'd talked more to her in that one night at the cabin, sitting in front of the fire and watching the meteor shower, than he had to anyone else in years.

A grin tugged at the corner of his lips thinking about that campfire and the sight of her bikini underwear going up in flames.

But it hadn't mattered how much fun they'd had, or the connection that he'd thought they felt.

She'd left anyway.

He couldn't blame her. Not after she'd overheard the conversation he'd had with the groom about how he didn't do relationships, and that he was supposed to have spent that weekend of the wedding hooking up with the *other* bridesmaid named Elizabeth instead of her.

At least she'd left a note. He'd read the thing so many times the edges were worn, and the envelope she'd written it on was bent from being tucked into his wallet for the last month.

It wasn't the first time he'd been dumped. He'd learned it was easier to be the first one to walk away—hurt less that way. But he'd felt something with Elizabeth, something different, something that made him think he might have a chance at that elusive happiness…and maybe even love. He'd sure thought he was falling at the time.

He stepped from the truck then held the door open for Dixie, his golden retriever, to jump out. She ran to the car in the driveway to sniff the tires, and he noted with a jolt that the compact white SUV was the same kind Elizabeth drove.

His chest tightened as his gaze jumped to the door of the house.

Could Elizabeth be here?

No way. What the hell would she be doing at the ranch next to his? She did have cousins all over the county. Maybe one of them had bought this farm.

Or maybe this car was just one of the million compact white SUV's out there, and he was just manifesting Elizabeth being here because she was on his mind. *Like usual.*

Dixie let out a bark and ran through the yard and up the rickety porch steps. The inside door was open, and the outer wooden screen door banged against the jamb as if being bumped against from the other side. A small yip came from inside the house then the screen door opened just enough for a small orange and white dog to squeeze through.

An orange and white dog that Ford recognized.

Thor.

There was no mistaking the dog. Elizabeth had told him it was a Havanese, and he'd never seen another one like it. And if there was any question that it was Elizabeth's dog, it would be squashed by the way the two dogs were racing around the yard together, tumbling over each other with excitement and recognition.

"Thor! Get back here!" a voice called from inside. A voice Ford had been hearing in his dreams. Obviously not the voice she was using to holler for the dog, but he knew it as well as he knew his own heart.

As if by their own volition, his feet started walking toward the house.

The screen door banged open. And then she was there—standing on the porch in a short white sun dress and high-heeled cowboy boots, her hair a mess of chestnut curls around her shoulders.

"Elizabeth," he breathed her name.

She froze, staring at him as if he were a mirage.

"Ford?" She took a step forward, her expression a mix of surprise and astonishment. "What are you doing he—?" she started to say as she took a step toward him.

Then a loud crack sounded as the old boards gave way, and she fell through the floor of the porch.

CHAPTER TWO

ELIZABETH COLE, AFFECTIONATELY known as Bitsy to her family, felt anything but 'bitsy' as her tall, curvy body crashed through the rotted floorboards of her new front porch.

There was close to a five-foot drop, and she cried out as first her knee then her hip then her forehead hit the jagged boards as she fell into the dark space. Her legs crumpled under her, and she shrieked at the feel of whispery legs skittering across her shins.

"Hold on," Ford called.

She could hear his bootheels racing across the sidewalk and up the steps. How in the heck was Ford Lassiter standing in her front yard? She hadn't seen the handsome cowboy since the morning she'd left a note and driven away from him and the small town of Creedence, where she'd been severely humiliated and had also had undoubtably the best, *and hottest*, weekend of her life.

The humiliation came from the fact that Ford had spent the weekend with *her* by mistake. He was meant to be set up with her gorgeous, and much more fun, cousin—also named Elizabeth. But the weekend they'd shared together had been glorious.

The time she'd spent with Ford and the way she'd stepped out of her comfort zone to be with him is what had given her the courage to make some huge changes in her life. Including buying this place.

This place that was literally falling down around her ears.

She waved her hands at the sticky spider webs trying to clutch at her clothes and hair and screamed as another creepy crawly skittered across her arm. The space under the porch was dark and damp, full of dead leaves and old boards.

Ford's strong hands reached down for her. His voice held a note of panic as he clasped her arms. "Are you okay? Are you hurt? Can you stand up?"

Stunned and hurt, she was trying to get her bearings as she struggled not to cry. Like, *really* struggled.

She swallowed around the huge lump in her throat. "I'm okay," she said, trying to keep her voice from wobbling. "I'm just embarrassed." She tried to get her feet under her. "And my knee hurts and my head hurts. And I think I scraped my arm." She didn't know what hurt more—the aches in her body, or her pride. Her voice rose as she slapped at her legs. "Holy crap! It feels like there's bugs crawling all over me."

"It's okay. I got you." Ford got a hold of her under her arms and hauled her up and out of the hole. She scrambled to gain purchase with her feet but leaned into him as he pulled her up. She hadn't seen him in weeks—was, in fact, a little mad at him—no, that didn't make sense, but she'd think about that later.

Right now, she was grateful for his strength and clung to his shoulders.

"Let's get you inside and assess the damage," Ford said, keeping his arm around her and carefully avoiding another hole in the porch boards as he opened the screen door and led her inside.

She'd bought the house 'as-is' which basically meant that she was stuck fixing everything and that no one had come in to remove all the discarded furniture. A small, ragged settee—that she already had big plans to recover—and an old farmhouse table with two mismatched chairs sat in the living area, and Ford led her to one of the chairs.

Sinking into it, she finally peered down at her legs to assess the damage…and saw an earwig stuck to her knee. At the same time, she felt something whispery on her arm and looked down to see a spider skittering across her forearm. And another one on the front of her dress. And another on her chest.

"Gah! Get them off me!" She pushed out of the chair and started limp-hopping around as she slapped at her arms and legs and the front of her dress. "Spiders! I hate spiders!" She couldn't see them, but she could feel them, and was sure they were in her clothes.

Her formerly white dress was covered in dirt and blood and something that looked like rust. And *so* many spiderwebs. She shrieked again as she saw a bug of some kind drop into her boot.

She had to get out of these clothes.

She didn't even think. She just grabbed the hem of her dress, hauled it over her head, and flung it on the floor. Hopping on one foot, she tried to get her boot off, but the damn thing was too tight. Why had she let that salesgirl talk her into these stupid boots anyway?

"Help me!" she cried to Ford. "There's a spider in my boot." Stars spun around her head as she bent forward, and a drop of blood hit the floor in front of her. She reached up to press her fingers to her throbbing head, but her forehead was damp and sticky.

Oh no. She didn't do well with blood. *Please don't be blood.*

She pulled her fingers away, and the room swam around her as she saw the bright red blood covering them. Her knees buckled and gave way under her.

From far away, she heard the sound of Ford's curse, then everything went black.

Ford blinked, frozen as he watched in astonishment as Elizabeth shrieked and slapped at herself then whipped her dress over her head and threw it on the floor.

He would have been more turned on by the sight of her in a black lacy bra and a pair of matching black lace panties, if it weren't for the blood dripping down her forehead, the big scrape on her knee, and the sight of another spider racing across her belly.

Then she touched her forehead. And he knew the second she saw the blood that she was going to faint.

"Holy shit," was all he got out as he took two

giant steps toward her and caught her before she hit the floor.

He stood there, holding the unconscious woman in his arms as he fervently looked around the room trying to figure out what the hell to do with her. She couldn't sit back in a chair, and that antique sofa was covered with so much dust and looked like it might crumple from any weight. He didn't have any other choice though. It was either the crappy sofa or the filthy floor.

Crappy sofa it is then.

He lifted her up and cradled her to his chest as he carried her to the sofa and gently set her down. Shaking the back, he tested its strength and was thankful that it was surprisingly sturdy.

Ford dropped to one knee to assess the damage. He lifted her chestnut blond bangs to get a better look at the cut on her forehead. It was still bleeding, but thankfully it was shallow and more of a scrape than a gash. The skin wasn't raised in a bump, which was also a good sign, but her fainting meant he couldn't rule out a concussion. He had a first aid kit in his truck, but he wasn't leaving her unconscious to go out and get it.

Another angry red scrape crossed her hip, and her knee was buggered up and bleeding too.

After making sure she was secure on the sofa, he hurried to the kitchen, praying the water was turned on and working. On the counter, next to a familiar pink tote bag, sat a turquoise stainless-steel water bottle, a plastic bucket filled with cleaning supplies, and a couple of large rolls of paper towels.

He shook his head as he wondered if Elizabeth

knew what kind of shape the house was in when she'd bought it. *If* she'd been the one who'd bought it. The realtor had said the owner had purchased it sight unseen, but if it *was* Elizabeth, she must not have expected *this* much damage if she'd only come prepared with a few rolls of paper towels and a bottle of Mountain Fresh-scented Pine Sol.

He turned on the faucet then tore off a few squares of paper towel as the pipes groaned then belched out a burst of rust-colored water. After a few spurts, the water flowed and finally ran clear. He wet the paper towels and grabbed the water bottle then hurried back to Elizabeth.

Thor and Dixie had been chasing each other around the room, occasionally stopping to wrestle then racing around again. The Golden had grabbed one edge of Elizabeth's dress, and the two dogs were now having a tug of war with it. A loud rip sounded as the fabric tore.

"Shit." Ford swore as he debated getting the dress back from the dogs—but stopping Elizabeth's head from bleeding seemed more pressing. He remembered how squeamish she was about blood. She'd nearly passed out the last time they were together and that was just from a skinned knee.

He knelt beside her and used the wet towels to wipe away the blood and dirt from her forehead and clean the wound. The bleeding had stopped, but dirt and dust rimmed the edges of the cut. *It's probably a good thing she's unconscious*, he thought as he poured more water from the water bottle onto the paper towels and thoroughly cleaned the cut.

Her eyelashes fluttered, and she winced as he

wiped away the rest of the dirt. She blinked at him, her expression confused, then her eyes widened, and she sat up and swiped at her arms and legs.

Ford grabbed for her hands, holding them firmly in his. "It's okay. There're no more spiders. You're safe."

Her shoulders slumped in relief then she looked down at herself, and her eyes widened again. "Oh my lanta," she cried, pulling her hands free and trying to cover herself. "How did I get on this sofa?"

Thor responded to her shriek by dropping the dress, leaping onto her lap, and trying to lick her chin. Dixie, never one to miss out on a chance at affection, raced to the sofa and tried to get in on the cuddle too.

"I carried you here when you fainted." Ford pulled Dixie back as he turned away, even though he'd already seen her in her underwear. And the sight of her wearing only a pair of cowboy boots with her black lace undies was already burned into his brain.

He stood and retrieved her dress, picking it up and shaking it out. He ran his hand over the fabric, checking to make sure it was free of bugs before he passed it to her. "It's still got some dust and blood on it, and some dog slobber, but the bugs should be gone."

She covered herself with the dress. "Oh my gosh. I'm so embarrassed. First, I fell through the porch, then I tore off my clothes, and then I fainted. You must think I'm a complete idiot."

"I don't think that at all," he assured her. "Anyone could have fallen through that floor. The porch has at least four holes in it, and the boards are practically rotted through. I'm just glad you didn't get more seriously hurt." He offered her a wry grin. "And I'll never complain about a woman tearing off her dress and tossing it at me."

A grin tugged at the corner of her lips. "I didn't toss it *at* you. I threw it on the floor. Then I *fainted*." She buried her face in her hands.

He knelt beside her and gently pulled her hands away, careful not to brush the scrape on her head. "I'm just glad you're okay." He passed her the water bottle. "Here, take a drink of this, then we need to get you cleaned up."

She took a sip then closed her eyes and dropped her chin to her chest.

Ford cupped her chin in his palm and gently lifted her head. "Come on now. Don't worry about it." He offered her a smile when she opened her eyes and looked at him. "Besides, it's not like I haven't already seen you in your underwear." He dropped his gaze to her lacy undies then quickly brought it back to meet her eyes. "Although it looks like these are an upgrade from the ones that got burnt up in our campfire."

A laugh escaped her lips. "They *are* an upgrade. I decided I never wanted to get caught in boring plain underwear again, so one of the first changes I made to the 'new' me was to buy fancier bras and undies."

He lifted one shoulder in a shrug. "I never considered your last underwear boring, although I'll admit it looked better on the floor than it did on you."

She snorted out another laugh then winced and

reached to touch her forehead. "Can we please stop talking about my underwear?"

"If we have to," he said.

She touched her forehead carefully then grimaced. "How bad is my head? Do I need to go to the emergency room to get stitches?" Her shoulders slumped again. "Shoot. I don't even know where the emergency room *is*. Does Woodland Hills even *have* a hospital?" She stared at the dilapidated room in front of her. "I haven't even been in this house an hour and it's already trying to kill me. Why did I think I could do this?"

It was Ford's turn to blink as Elizabeth leapt from one conversation subject to another in rapid-fire succession. "What do you mean? Are you really the one who bought this house?"

She nodded, her expression grim, as she dropped her gaze. A small spider crawled out of her boot and toward her knee. She shrieked and kicked her leg out, the toe of her boot catching him on the chin and knocking him backwards.

CHAPTER THREE

ELIZABETH WATCHED IN horror as Ford fell backwards and landed on his butt. She couldn't believe she'd just kicked him in the face.

Then the spider skittered against her skin, and her focus shifted back to her boot. She tried to yank it off, but the dang thing was stuck. "Help me," she begged.

Ford shook his head, looking a little dazed as he rubbed his chin, but God love him, he hauled himself to his knees, grabbed the heel of her boot, and pulled. Her foot finally released the devil's footwear, and he flung it behind him as he reached for her other boot and tugged it off too.

She wrenched off her socks, tossed them across the room, then furiously brushed her hands over her feet, making sure there were no more bugs or spiders on her skin.

Ford was still on his knees, and despite having her just kicked him in the face, he still offered her a cocky grin. "Anything else you want me to help you take off?"

She huffed out a laugh as she shook her head. "No, that's enough. Thank you."

"You sure there's not a bug in your bra? You could take it off too—just to be sure."

She peered into her cleavage as she pressed a hand to her chest. "Oh my gosh. Don't even joke about that." Suddenly realizing just how much cleavage she had on display, thanks to her lacy push-up bra, she pulled the edge of her dress up to her chin.

"Sorry, that wasn't kind of me," he said. "I was just teasing. But I think you've been through enough bug and spider trauma." He peered down at her knee. "I've got a first aid kit in my truck. How about I grab that and give you a chance to get dressed?"

She nodded and pushed herself up then fell back as a wave of dizziness struck.

"Whoa there," he said, leaning forward to cup her elbow and gently pull her to him. "Take it easy sitting up. You bumped your head *and* fainted. I think I've got some ibuprofen in my glove box. I'll bring you some of that too. But don't try to stand until I get back."

"Okay," she told him as she swung her legs over the seat and pressed her hands into the sofa to steady herself.

"Take another drink," he said, pressing the water bottle into her hands. "I'll be right back." He stood and strode out of the house, mindful of the hole in the porch as he let the screen door bang behind him.

Elizabeth took another sip, the water cooling her parched throat. She set the bottle next to her then unfurled her dress and shook it out one more time, just to be sure it was truly bug and spider-free, before pulling it back over her head. She wiggled the bodice down then tried to pull the skirt over her knees without standing up, a task that worked semi-okay since there was a big hole in the middle of the dress where the skirt had been torn away at the waist.

What the heck?

Had she ripped her dress when she'd thrown it across the room?

Ford came back in, carrying a small blue plastic case and a bottle of ibuprofen. He knelt in front of her and handed her the bottle as he nodded at her bare midriff visible through the hole in her dress. "Sorry about that. I think the dogs got ahold of it while I was trying to clean up your head."

"Sounds about par for the course for my day," she told him as she tried, and failed, to unscrew the child-proof cap.

He took the bottle back from her, opened the lid and shook two capsules into her hand. She washed them down with more water as he opened the first aid kit and dug through its contents. "Looks like I've got some antibiotic ointment and some Band-Aids." He gingerly pulled her knee toward him and studied the scrape. "I need to wash this out first though." He poured some water from her bottle onto the cut, and she inhaled through her teeth at the sting. "Sorry darlin', I know that's gotta hurt. I'm almost done."

"I'm okay," she said, gripping the sides of the settee as he used some gauze from the first aid kit to clean the remaining dirt from the wound.

His hands were gentle, and even though nothing about her sitting in front of him in a filthy blood-and-dirt-stained dress while he squeezed antibiotic ointment onto her scraped up knee would be considered sexy, she couldn't help but remember the way his hands had felt as they'd grazed over her naked skin.

He stuck a Band-aid on her knee then slid his hand up her thigh. "We need to take care of that one on your hip too."

Oh. My.

If his hand on her knee was already giving her tingles in her lady parts, how was she going to be able to handle his fingertips grazing over her bare hip? She sucked her bottom lip under her top teeth as the memories of their two glorious nights together earlier that summer came flooding back to her.

Not that those memories were ever far away. She'd thought about—or more accurately—tried *not* to think about Ford Lassiter every day since she'd driven away from him, leaving him with only a note to say goodbye. She probably hadn't handled that the best way, but she'd been so hurt, so crushed, when she'd overheard him talking to her cousin, Brody, and realized he thought he'd been set up that weekend with someone else.

She'd spent that entire weekend stepping out of her comfort zone, trying new things, and pretending she was a different Elizabeth. An Elizabeth who didn't have a cutesy nickname, and a cruddy third-floor apartment, and a job working for her parents. An Elizabeth who wasn't afraid to take chances, to make risky moves, to see a photo of an old farmhouse in a realtor's window and make a snap decision to purchase it without ever seeing it in person.

She touched the pendant at her neck—a sterling silver shooting star with a sparkly gem at its center.

Ford had given her the necklace that last morning. He'd told her he'd picked it up on a whim at the general store because it made him think of her. She'd gotten teary-eyed when he'd given it to her. Not just because he'd thought of her and bought her a gift, but because he told her the necklace was a souvenir of the meteor shower they'd stayed up half the night watching and a reminder to go for the things she wanted, and that she could get them just by doing one brave thing at a time.

She'd done something brave, she'd made a bold step, and plunked down the majority of her savings on a down payment for this farm, promising her dog, the only male in her life who'd always been there for her, a better life.

When she'd made that promise, she'd envisioned the tidy green lawn and flower gardens behind the white picket fence in the realtor's photo. She'd imagined raising chickens and taking Thor for long walks in the pastures then spending their evenings hanging out on the wrap-around porch sipping lemonade and watching the sunset.

She sure hadn't imagined that the porch would have several holes in it and be made of rotted wood. She hadn't imagined the weed-filled lawn that hadn't seen grass in what looked like years. Or that the chicken coop would be falling down.

Ford gently brushed the hem of her dress to the side so he could wash out and bandage the scrape on her hip, but instead of relishing the feel of his strong hand on her skin, she looked around the house at the faded wallpaper and the chipped and stained linoleum kitchen floor. She noted the ancient, yellowed refrigerator and stove and the absence of a dishwasher.

And the upstairs had been just as bad.

What had she been thinking?

The enormity of the work ahead of her—just to make this place livable—filled her with anxiety, and she choked back a sob.

Ford had just been securing a Band-aid on her hip, and his head snapped up. "Hey now. It's okay. Was I hurting you? I'm so sorry."

"No, it wasn't you," she said, brushing away the lone tear that had escaped her eye. "It's this place. I had no idea how much work it needed. It doesn't look anything like the pictures."

He kept his hand on her hip as he let out a sigh. "So, you really did buy this place?"

"Yep. Just signed the closing docs this morning. The ink is barely dry on the check."

"Dang." He let out a low whistle. "I hope you got a good deal."

"I did. Which should have been my first clue that it was too good to be true."

"Didn't you want to at least see it?"

"I thought I had with the pictures. I just didn't know the pictures must be from a decade ago. And I'm realizing now that I probably should have hired my own inspector and had him drive up from Denver rather than rely on some guy named Charlie that the realtor recommended."

Ford nodded. "Charlie Danvers is a heck of a nice guy. But he's pushing eighty, and I can't imagine his eyesight's as good as it used to be. Plus, he's of the age and mindset that most things can be patched up or put back together with a little bailing wire and some gumption."

She let out a small laugh. "Yes, I believe those were his exact words to me when he called and talked me through the inspection. He told me overall the place was in good shape, it just needed some fresh paint, new appliances, and a few repairs, but nothing that couldn't be fixed right up with a little elbow grease and some gumption."

"I think this place is gonna take more than a little elbow grease."

"And now I'm starting to wonder if that realtor is setting me up again."

"What do you mean?"

"She sent a contractor out here about an hour ago. A guy named Chad Duchon or Duchet or douche-something, and he spent five minutes walking through the place and told me he'd be back with a written quote, but his initial estimate was equal to the price I paid for the house."

"That's Chad Ducette, but douche-something works just as well. The guy's a blowhard."

"That's one way to put it. He made me feel like he'd be doing me a favor to take thousands of dollars from me, and I'm not sure the guy could pick me out of a line-up because his eyes never rose above my neck."

Ford's jaw twitched at her comment. "You're *not* using that guy." His tone came out hard and demanding, but he must have realized it because he cleared his throat then softened it. "I mean, you don't have to use that guy for your renovations."

"This is a small town. I'm not sure there will be a

lot of choices. The realtor told me they were going to send out another guy, some rancher who lives near here, but he hasn't shown up yet, so I may be stuck with the overpriced douche-canoe who was more interested in my cleavage than my construction needs."

"The other guy *did* show up."

Elizabeth turned her head to look out the big bay window, one of the things she *did* love about the house. "When? Did you see him? Why didn't he stay?"

"He did. He hauled you out of the porch and just bandaged your scraped knee."

CHAPTER FOUR

ELIZABETH GASPED. "YOU?"

Ford nodded.

"But the realtor said it was someone local. Someone who lived on a ranch near here."

Ford nodded again. "Yeah, that's me. The Lassiter Ranch is right up the road. You probably passed the sign on your way here."

She'd been so focused on getting to the house she hadn't paid any attention to the surrounding area. "But you don't live *here*. You live in Creedence."

"No. The wedding was in Creedence, but I live here."

"But you went to school with my cousin, Brody. In Creedence." She couldn't wrap her mind around this. She hadn't really bought the house *right next door* to the guy she'd had a wedding one-night—er, make that *two*-night—stand with.

"Yeah, we *all* went to school in Creedence. All the kids from Creedence, Woodland Hills and the next town over, all went to school together. And our graduating class still only totaled about eighty kids."

"I didn't know. I swear I didn't know. I never

would have bought this place if I would have known you lived next door."

He grimaced. "I'm not *that* bad of a neighbor."

"No, of course not, I didn't mean…" she backpedaled. "I just meant that after we, you know, I wasn't like stalking you, or expecting anything from you."

"No," he said, his expression darkening as he stood up. "You made that quite clear in your note."

Her shoulders sunk inward. That note *had* been the coward's way out. But she just couldn't face Ford. She was too humiliated. And she'd heard her cousin say that Ford didn't do commitment and was only looking for someone to have a good time with. Which told her that all the chemistry she'd thought they'd had together had only been in the physical sense. And all the connections she'd thought they'd had had only been one-sided.

"Ford, listen—" she started to say, but he held up his hand.

"I don't think you should beat yourself up too much about this house," he said, acting like the other conversation, the one they *should* be having, didn't exist. "It's got good bones. And Charlie was right about a fresh coat of paint. That will make a world of difference."

"Are you really the person the realtor sent out to help me with the renovations?"

He nodded. "I told you that my brothers and I helped fix up that old hunting cabin. I can do pretty much everything you need. And if I don't know how to do it, I'll bet I know a guy who does. And it isn't Chad Douche-Nugget."

She swallowed at the memory of their night at the hunting cabin and waking up naked and wrapped around each other in the back of his pickup. Pushing the thoughts from her mind, she tried to focus on the task at hand.

Except she didn't really know what tasks *were* at hand.

"Honestly, I have no idea what I'm doing. I've watched a lot of HGTV and Fixer Upper, and I do have some ideas of what I'd *like* to do, but I have no clue if those ideas are even feasible or if I can afford them or if they would even work."

Ford walked back to her and held out his hand. "Why don't we walk through the house together. You can tell me what you're thinking, and I'll give you an idea what'll work and what won't."

Okay. Apparently, they weren't going to talk about the wedding weekend at all right now. Which was fine with her.

She pushed up from the settee and tested her knee. It was sore, but she could walk. The giant rip at her waist was another matter. She twisted the fabric together and held it as she padded barefoot across the floor.

Ford stopped her again. "You can't be walking around here without any shoes on. Even if you have had a recent Tetanus shot."

She looked at the stupid high-heeled boots Ford had tossed on the floor. "Well, I'm not putting those suckers back on. I've only been wearing them a few hours, and they've already been giving me blisters. I can't believe I let that shopgirl talk me into buying them. I just wanted to look like I fit in. Like I could be a woman who owned a farm."

"Those aren't the kind of boots you need to run a farm. You need some that can get muddy and are comfortable and will protect your feet. We can check in at the mercantile downtown later and find you some Ropers." He frowned at her bare feet. "Do you have any other shoes to wear?"

"I brought my suitcase and some of my things. I was planning to sleep here tonight, but now that I've seen the house, I think I'll probably end up getting a room at the hotel."

Ford made a growling sound as he headed for the door. "I'll grab your suitcase."

"I can get it," she said, padding after him.

He pointed at the floor. "You stay here so you don't add a nail to the foot to your current injuries. It'll just take me a sec."

He had a point.

"Thank you. If you can just grab the blue tote bag, that would be all I need. It's on the floor of the passenger seat. I brought some grubbies to wear to clean in."

It only took him a minute, then he was back, carrying her blue tote in his hand. She set it on the sofa and dug out her jean shorts, a pale blue tank top, and a pair of Chaco sandals. Ford turned his back as she hiked up the shorts then pulled the dress off and the tank top on. Not that it mattered. He'd already seen her in her underwear.

But she still appreciated the gesture.

She shoved her feet into the sandals and left the torn and filthy dress on the sofa. "I brought a notebook with me to start a list of projects. And I knew I'd want to paint and maybe upgrade the floor, so I have a bunch of paint sample cards and some flooring samples, too."

"Great. Grab all that. We can start down here then move upstairs." He pointed to the floor. "This is all the original hardwood. If you like the look of it, I'd say it's still in pretty good shape. It wouldn't take much to sand it and add a new coat of stain and sealer. You'd be amazed at the difference. And it wouldn't cost much to do it."

"I love these floors," she told him. "And I love *anything* that won't cost much to do."

"I know it looks like a mess in here, but the house has good bones and if you like some of the original stuff and aren't afraid of getting your hands dirty, I think you could save a lot by keeping or refurbishing most of it."

"I'm afraid of a lot of things, but hard work isn't one of them," she told him. "And I've got the time right now to do it. I'm still doing my parent's books, and I kept most of my CPA clients, but I'll be working remotely now, so my schedule is more flexible. And I told all of them that I was taking the next few weeks off to focus on the house."

"Good. This will take more than a few weeks to finish, but you'll be amazed at how much can be accomplished in a short amount of time. Especially if you're helping." He led her into the kitchen. "I know the cabinets look a little shabby, but they're oak and still solid. You could save a *lot* of money by not having to buy new cabinets. We could paint these and add new hardware, and they'd look fresh and updated and still keep that farmhouse feel."

"I was already thinking about that. I'd love to paint the ones on top a creamy white and the ones on the bottom a deep navy blue, then add brushed nickel handles. I plan to spend a lot of time in the kitchen, so I've already budgeted for new appliances and quartz countertops."

"I like your color choices, and they'd work well with the oak flooring. Add in a new sink and faucet, and this kitchen will look brand new. And won't take that long to complete."

The main floor of the house was a large living area separated by a kitchen island. A small half-bath was on this level along with a mudroom off the kitchen that had a door leading to the backyard.

Elizabeth led Ford through a set of French doors into the room in the tower. "This is my favorite room," she told him. "I want to make this an office with my desk looking out toward the mountains. I can already see myself working in here."

Ford studied the room. "You could paint in here right away then throw down a rug and you'd be ready to work."

A feeling like hope bloomed in Elizabeth's chest. Maybe she *could* make this work.

The upstairs held four small bedrooms, two on each side of a long hallway with another bathroom at the end.

"We'd need to check with a structural engineer," Ford said, standing in the largest bedroom after having already poked his head into the other three. "But I'd bet we could knock down the wall between this room and the one next to it, or at least create an arched opening, to turn this into a master suite."

"I'd love that," Elizabeth said. When she'd looked upstairs before, she'd only seen faded wallpaper, dinghy paint, and tiny closets. The windows were so filthy that they didn't let much light in, but now, with Ford's sharp eye for detail, she noticed the antique light fixtures and the potential of the wainscoting.

"Did you see the master bathroom?" he asked, leading her toward a door she hadn't noticed before. "We knew the folks who lived here before, and I remember Frank had this built for his wife as a gift for their fiftieth wedding anniversary."

She shook her head then gasped as she followed him through the doorway. The bathroom was in the corner tower part of the house and even though one of the windows was broken and boarded up and the black-and-white-checked tile floor was filthy, the room was still gorgeous.

Double sinks sat on top of a vanity made from what looked like an antique dresser. A huge mirror flanked by cream and gold sconces hung on the wall above it. Vintage floral wallpaper in shades of periwinkle blue and white covered the top half of the wall and white beadboard covered the bottom.

But the piece de resistance was the huge white clawfoot bathtub that sat in front of the windows. Granted, the tub was as grubby as the floor, but she could fix that.

"I love this so much," she said, already imagining herself surrounded by candles as she soaked in the tub full of bubbles. An image of Ford sitting across from her in the tub filled her mind, and she turned to look out the window, as if he might notice the sudden heat rising up her neck.

"Tub looks big enough for two," he said, his voice low and closer behind her than she'd thought.

"Those two sure seem to be enjoying it," she said with a shiver as she pointed to a spider dangling from the faucet and another on the other side of the tub. Easier to make a joke than respond to his…what was that…an offer? Or just an observation?

"What did you think of the attic room?" he asked as they made their way back through the bedroom.

"What attic room?"

"The one above the bathroom."

"I didn't even realize there was another floor."

He led her into the hallway and opened a small door farther down. It was narrower than the bedroom doors and had an antique crystal doorknob.

"I thought that was a linen closet," she said, peering up the narrow staircase.

"I don't know how often Frank and Ida got up in here in their later years, but we used to love to play up here."

She followed Ford up the stairs, noting how great his butt looked in his jeans. Excitement and apprehension filled her at the thought of an attic room in the tower. Her mind filled with visions of antique trunks stuffed with vintage dresses and forgotten love letters then switched to images of ghosts haunting the old rafters.

"Please don't let us find a dead body up here," she muttered.

Ford stopped at the top of the stairs and turned

back to her, an amused expression on his face. "A dead body? That was dark."

"Maybe," she said, with a shrug. "But do you have an idea how many books I've read where the unsuspecting city girl buys a fixer-upper in a small town only to discover a corpse in the attic, or the basement, or the walls, of her new house?"

He let out a soft chuckle then continued up the stairs. "I think you're in the clear so far. No dead bodies. Just a bunch of old books."

"*Old books?*" Her pulse raced, and she practically knocked him over in her haste to get to the top of the stairs. Then she grabbed his arm, her breath caught in her throat as she froze, her eyes going wide as she peered into the round room.

CHAPTER FIVE

FORD COULDN'T HELP the smile that crept over his face as he watched Elizabeth's sheer joy as she stared around the attic room. He remembered helping his grandfather and Frank build the floor to ceiling bookshelves that circled the room on either side of the double bay windows.

Ida had begged Frank to turn the tower room into a library, and she'd practically swooned at the sight of the spacious window seat they'd also built. Kind of like Elizabeth was doing now.

Her mouth hung open in awe as she stepped into the room, her gaze bouncing from the stacks of paperbacks piled haphazardly on the floor to the rows of leatherbound hardbacks lining a few of the dusty shelves. Most of the six bookcases were empty, but some still held books from various decades.

"Oh my gosh," Elizabeth kept whispering, over and over, as she flitted from shelf to shelf, discovering a new treasured book every few seconds. "This is amazing." She held up a dusty book. "*The Great Gatsby.* It's one of my favorite books."

She didn't seem to notice the stale, musty scent or

the spiderwebs in the corners of the rafters. Or the dust covering every surface.

She reverently held the book to her chest and plopped down on the window seat. A cloud of dust rose around her perfectly shaped bottom. Not that he'd been looking at her butt. Not in the last few seconds anyway.

"This room is *everything*," she said, her voice an emotion-filled whisper. She turned to him, and he was overcome at the well of tears shining in her eyes. "I can do this. Right? I didn't just make the worst mistake of my life, did I? I *can* make a life here."

"Sure. You can do whatever you want."

She patted the seat next to her and another puff of dust rose in the air. "What if I'm not entirely sure what it is that I want?" She stared up at the ceiling. "I just know I didn't want the life I had."

He sat next to her, oblivious to the dust but all too aware of the floral scent coming off her skin in the warm attic. He breathed it in, remembering the way she'd smelled, the way she'd felt in his arms, the small sighs she'd made as he'd kissed her sweet-smelling neck.

Letting out his breath, he tried to regain his focus. "What was it that made you buy this house?"

Both dogs had come up the stairs after them and were sniffing the stacks of books and old papers. Satisfied once they'd investigated every square inch of the round room, Thor stretched out in a patch of sun, and Dixie padded over and sat by their feet. She rested her head on Elizabeth's knee, and Ford reached over and peeled a string of cobwebs from the side of her ear.

Elizabeth absently scratched Dixie's neck as she let out a long heavy breath. "I don't know, really. I know I wanted—no, *needed*—a change, needed to do something, to take a risk."

He huffed out a laugh as he gestured around the room. "This was risky, all right."

She shook her head. "I don't know how to explain it. It wasn't *just* about taking a risk. It was more like finally being brave enough to take that first step to making a change in my life. You know, I told you how scared I was to step out of my comfort zone." Ford noted that she absently fingered the shooting star pendant as she spoke.

He couldn't believe that she'd not only *kept* the necklace he'd given her, but that she'd worn it on the day she made what sounded like one of the biggest changes of her life. He'd noticed it earlier when he was carrying her to the sofa, and the sight of it around her neck made something in his chest ache.

"I saw a flyer for this place in the real estate agency's window that weekend of the wedding. And I could just *see* myself living there. Me and Thor." She smiled over at the dog, then her smile turned shy as she looked back at him. "I took a lot of chances that weekend, acted out of character for me. But this place, that picture, I don't know, something about it just called to me. And after everything that had happened that weekend, I suddenly found the courage to take one step, to do *one* brave thing. Granted it was a heck of a thing. But I stopped in that real estate office on my way out of town and made an offer that day."

He let out a low whistle. "Just like that?"

She nodded and another smile tugged at her lips, this one different though. She smiled as if she had a secret, or that she'd done something she was proud of. "Just like that. You know I'm an accountant, so of course, I had the down payment. I'd been saving for a house for years. Although I don't think this house is what I imagined when I opened that savings account all those years ago."

"No, I wouldn't think so," he said, imagining her plunking down her savings for a practical tri-level on a tree-lined street.

"When I told my family what I'd done, they all freaked out and told me what an idiot I was, which just made me dig my heels in more and stand by my decision. And everything happened so fast. In the space of a few weeks, I was essentially quitting my job and leaving the family business and trying to pack my apartment and get out of my lease, and order furniture, which all probably contributed to the fact that I trusted the realtor *and* the inspector she hired and closed on this place without ever even driving up here to see it."

"I wondered about that. Seems like you would have at least wanted to check it out for yourself."

"Part of me did. But another part of me just wanted to believe in the adventure and the magic of that spontaneous half-crazy, half-courageous decision to buy the place. I looked at that picture, and I *wanted* to live here. I wanted *us* to live here."

Ford's chest tightened at the idea of the two of them living on this farm together. But surprisingly not in a totally bad way. His mind went to visions of him and Elizabeth sitting on the porch like Frank and Ida had, two glasses of lemonade and a plate of homemade cookies between them. He turned to her and saw she was smiling down at the dog again and then realized her 'us' had meant she and the dog, not and she and *him*.

Oh well. He didn't like lemonade all that much anyway.

Oblivious to his sudden 'them living here and growing old together' fantasy, Elizabeth kept talking. "You remember I told you how I traded my apartment to my neighbor in exchange for Thor?"

"Yeah."

"When I did that, I promised him that he'd have a good life with me. A better life than he'd had with her. And I thought this farm was my chance to give it to him."

"So, you bought this old run-down farm as a gift for your dog?"

She let out a small laugh. "I guess. But also, as a gift to myself. The gift of a new life. And remember, I didn't know it was an old run-down farm until I drove up to it a few hours ago."

"So, what do you think now?"

"I don't know. I'm probably still in shock, and remember, I *did* bump my head, but I actually kind of love it. Even though it's probably going to cost me way more than I'd planned to fix it up, and I brought the wrong kind of boots for a farm, and I don't even own a hammer, I'm really kind of excited to dig in and start working on this house."

"I'll remind you of that when your back is killing

you and you've got paint in your hair for the fifth day in a row."

She laughed and something in his chest eased. He loved the sound of her laughter and dug it even more when he was the one responsible for making her laugh.

"Seriously though," she said, turning to him and resting a hand on his arm. "I'm impressed with your ideas, and you obviously know what you're doing. If you're serious about helping me do the renovations, I would love to hire you. I'm not made of money, and it sounds like I'm probably already in over my head with this place, so I'd love to do as much of it myself as I can. And I don't expect any favors because of…you know…our history. This is business, and I would pay you a fair price."

He nodded. "This is a side gig for me, so I don't charge as much as someone like the douche-canoe would. And he'd probably upcharge you for the subcontractors he'd bring in too. I'm just the one guy, so I'd do the work of the contractor *and* the subs. I can write you up a quote of the things I would need to cover then include a list of optional items you can either tackle yourself or pay me to do. Or hire someone else to do."

"That sounds perfect."

"We've already talked through a lot of the stuff you want to do, but we can work on a more comprehensive plan and start a list of all the supplies we'll need. Our local lumberyard should carry most of what you need, and we have a pretty good hardware store. You can probably save a little by ordering some things, like the sink and some of the fixtures, and I'm sure you can get your appliances delivered. When were you wanting to start?"

"Considering I've already moved out of my apartment and had been planning to begin sleeping here tonight, I'm gonna say the sooner the better. How does tomorrow work for you?"

"Tomorrow works just fine." His heart jumped in his chest at the thought that Elizabeth Cole was moving in next door to him. And that he was going to be working with her every day.

Damn. Calm down son.

He felt like a teenage boy—getting all squirrelly around the pretty girl. He needed to cut that crap out. *Now.* He did *not* get squirrelly over pretty girls.

Not anymore.

He'd learned the hard way that falling in love only led to heartbreak. And that he wasn't the kind of guy people stuck around for. Not his daddy, or his mother, or the one girl he'd let himself fall in love with all those years ago…they'd all eventually left him behind.

And looking at the woman sitting next to him right now—even though she had a smudge of dirt on her chin and a Band-aid on her forehead—he'd felt things for her, things that he hadn't felt for another woman in a long time. Things he couldn't let himself feel again, because this woman, the one still wearing the dime-store necklace he'd bought her a month ago, she'd already left him once. And he knew if he let himself really fall for her—she had the ability to break him.

He swallowed then cleared his throat. "There's plenty to start on, just in cleaning the place up and prepping to paint. And I'll get that hole in the porch fixed first thing. At least make it safe to walk across." He frowned. "Were you really planning to sleep here tonight?"

She nodded. "I've got a sleeping bag and an air mattress in the back of my car. I imagined it would be kind of like camping. But at least here there would be bathrooms."

"Assuming the plumbing works."

She groaned. "Please tell me the plumbing works."

He chuckled. "Why don't you go downstairs and get some of those paint samples out. I'll check on the upstairs plumbing, and I want to look at a couple of the windows. Then I'll come down, and we can start working on that supply list." He checked his watch, surprised that it was already past six. "The hardware store's closed for the night, but we can be armed and ready to hit it first thing in the morning."

Elizabeth couldn't help smiling as she walked down the stairs. *Her* stairs.

She ran her hand along the banister, then jerked it back as a splinter bit into her palm. Okay, so it wasn't perfect. It was way far from perfect.

But it was hers.

And there was something so exciting about the idea of taking this rundown farmhouse and fixing it up. Of picking the paint colors she wanted. Of sanding *her* floors and helping to restore them to their once gorgeous shine.

There was also something *really* exciting about

doing it all with Ford Lassiter. She could ignore the fact that she was going to pay him to help her and just focus on the idea that he was going to be *here* in this house with her, working beside her every day. She was going to get to admire the arm-porn of his muscular forearms and watch him stride around wearing a tool-belt and swinging a hammer. And it was summer, so maybe it would be so hot that he'd have to take his shirt off to work.

Whew. She'd already seen the man naked, and she was getting hot just thinking about seeing his bare chest again.

Using her fingernail, she dug the splinter from her palm as she descended the last few stairs.

Then her injured hand flew to her mouth to stifle a scream at the huge man standing in the middle of her living room.

CHAPTER SIX

ELIZABETH STARED AT the man, her mouth dry as she prepared to fight or take flight. Her gaze traveled around the room looking for something to use as a weapon to defend herself.

"What are you doing in my house?" she finally managed to say.

Chad Douche-Nugget leaned casually against the kitchen counter, completely oblivious to the fact that he'd just scared the hell out of her. Or maybe that was his intent.

She took a few wary steps into the living room, mentally measuring if her escape route should be out the front door to her car or back up the steps toward Ford.

Funny, she hadn't felt scared, even for a second, being alone and out in the country with Ford all afternoon. In fact, he'd made her feel safe and taken care of as he'd cleaned and bandaged her wounds.

But this man, this random arrogant contractor that she'd met earlier that day, who had *let himself into her home*, this guy scared her. She couldn't pinpoint exactly what it was—maybe it was the cocky way he grinned at her or the predatory gleam in his eye—

but something about him raised the hair on the back of her neck.

"Hey now," he said. "Is that any way to greet your new hero?"

"My hero? How do you figure?"

He lifted one shoulder in a shrug. "I'm the guy who's going to fix this dump up. And I was thinking a girl like you might want to show her appreciation by..." He paused as if letting the words settle in the room.

"A girl like *me*?" She huffed. "What's that supposed to mean?"

Did he mean a girl who was smart and had a college degree? Or one who was quick-witted and knew how to deliver a punchline? Or did he mean a girl like her who was curvy and a little soft in the belly—who he must think is so desperate for a man that she would fall all over herself to jump into bed with any conceited A-hole who offered to repair her flooring?

He shrugged again but he let his gaze run over her body, lingering on her ample hips.

Steam practically shot out of her ears as she planted a fist on one of those ample hips. "Well, I'm sorry to inform you, Chad, but your services won't actually be needed here. Not as a contractor or as any other services you think you might be able to provide."

His expression darkened as his brow furrowed. "What are you talking about? You already hired me this morning."

"No. I didn't. I just asked you to provide me with a quote. And it turns out that I won't need one from you after all."

"You can't do that," he said, taking a step toward her. "We had a deal. And besides, I'm the only real contractor in this county. Who are you going to get to do the kind of work I do? My prices might be a little high. But I'm worth it." He slid into sleazy car-salesman mode again, lifting his chin toward her as his gaze dipped to her chest. "And maybe we can work out a deal where I knock off a little if you show me some of that appreciation we were talking about."

This guy was really starting to creep her out. He didn't seem to want to take no for an answer. She had to say something that would get him out of her house. And out of her life.

"You were the only one talking about that. And frankly, I don't appreciate what you're insinuating, and *my boyfriend* wouldn't appreciate it either."

"Boyfriend?" he scoffed.

Yes. *Scoffed.* This jerk had the gall to scoff at her—like someone *like her* couldn't have a boyfriend.

"Yeah. *Serious* boyfriend."

She didn't know where this was coming from. But she figured the only way she was going to get this guy to leave her alone was by claiming there was another alpha male in the picture. One who could kick his conceited butt to the curb.

"And he's the one who's going to fix this place up," she added. Then just to throw a little salt in the wound, she threw his earlier declaration back at him. "He's my *real* hero."

He huffed out a disdainful laugh. "Yeah, I bet. The guy probably can't even swing a hammer. Where is this *supposed* boyfriend anyway?"

"I'm right here," a deep voice said from the stairwell.

Then Elizabeth almost fainted again as Ford strolled into the room and slung his arm around her shoulders. He pulled her close and pressed a quick kiss to her lips. "Sorry about that, darlin'. I didn't know we had company. I would have come downstairs sooner."

"Th-that's okay," she stammered, her lips tingling from his kiss. His voice sounded casual, but she could feel the tenseness in his shoulders and the slight tremble of his hand as he gripped her arm—as if he were barely containing his anger. "Do you know Chad Douche…ette?"

"I do," Ford said, his voice steely as he stepped forward to extend his hand. "But not well enough that he lets himself into my house."

Elizabeth's eyes widened at the force in which Ford gripped Chad's hand.

"*Your* house?" Chad asked, extricating his hand from the other man's grip. "I thought this was *her* house. And you're telling you're *her* boyfriend?"

"Sure am," Ford said, his tone still hard as he stepped back to wrap his arm possessively around Elizabeth's waist. His fingers dug into her hip, he was holding her so tightly. "Have been for some time now. In fact, I'm going to be moving in here with her. And *I'll* be doing the renovations. So, like she said, we won't be needing you. And I don't appreciate the way you're talking to my girl, so I'm gonna ask you to leave now." He narrowed his eyes further. "And I'm only going to ask once."

Chad's chest puffed out, and he opened his mouth

like he was about to say something else, but Ford took a menacing step toward him, and he must have decided against it. He waved his hand dismissively at Elizabeth. "Whatever," he muttered. "I don't need this stupid job anyway."

He turned, but only got a few steps before Ford strode past him and blocked the front door. Chad was tall, but Ford was taller, and his body pulsed with rage as he reached out, grabbed the contractor by the collar, and hauled Chad to his chest.

Ford stared hard into the other man's eyes, his jaw tense. "Don't you *ever* let yourself into this house again. In fact, don't ever *speak* to Elizabeth again. You see her coming, you walk the other direction. You get me?"

Chad shot a glare at Elizabeth then gave a short tight nod to Ford.

"Now get the hell off our property," Ford said, pushing open the door and throwing Chad out.

The other man stumbled as he tried to avoid the hole in the porch then righted himself and stomped down the stairs, shoving the porch railing loose as he went. It toppled into the dirt.

"I'll send you a bill for that," Ford called to him.

Chad ignored him as he got into his truck, slammed the door, then sent gravel flying as he peeled out of the driveway.

Ford's body was shaking as he strode back to Elizabeth. "That took everything I had not to punch that conceited asshole in the throat." He softened his tone and expression as he took her by the shoulders. "Are you okay? He didn't touch you, did he?"

She shook her head, too stunned by Ford's reaction

to say anything. He was *pissed*. But was he really this angry because of the way Chad treated her? Or did he just not like the guy in general?

"Shit," he said, letting out his breath and scrubbing his hand across the whiskers on his jaw. "I'm sorry. I don't know why I said all that. That guy just made me so frickin' mad. I heard the way he was talking to you, and I couldn't let that stand."

"It's okay. I appreciated it."

"Did you know he was coming over here?"

"No. I just walked down the stairs, and he was standing in the kitchen. Scared the heck out of me. My phone was in my purse, and he was standing between me and the door. And then the stuff he was saying was really starting to freak me out. I hadn't really thought about how isolated I would be out in the country." She pressed a hand to her heart as she imagined what could have happened. "I've never had an unwanted man in my house like that. I mean, sure I've had my landlord stop by, but he never made leering remarks or insinuated that I should offer him sexual favors for fixing the garbage disposal."

A growl sounded in the back of Ford's throat as his hands tightened into fists. "On second thought, I *should* have punched that guy."

"No. You handled it just right. Getting him out of the house and discouraging him from coming back was what I was trying to do. He just wasn't getting the hint from me."

"That's what I was trying to do, too." He frowned. "But I probably shouldn't have told him I was moving in here. I don't know what I was thinking. I guess I wasn't. Thinking, I mean. I just reacted. But

I didn't want *him* thinking you would be out here alone or that he could come back by when I wasn't here."

"I appreciate that. And I was doing the same thing by telling him I had a boyfriend."

Ford's lips pulled together as he eyed her. "Do you?"

"Do I what?"

"Have a boyfriend?"

A nervous giggle bubbled out of her. Dang. She'd forgotten how many times that had happened to her the last time she'd been with Ford. "No. I do *not* have a boyfriend."

She liked the way his lip twitched, as if he were trying not to smile. He cocked an eyebrow and offered her a sheepish grin. "Well, apparently, you do now."

CHAPTER SEVEN

WHAT THE HELL had he just done?
Ford was going for funny, trying to make a joke, but he feared that came out a little more serious sounding than he'd meant for it to.

Especially since Elizabeth's eyes just went round, and she gave another one of those little giggles that he knew happened when she was nervous.

"At least as far as Chad's concerned, I mean," he said, trying to backpedal.

The sparkle in her eyes dimmed a little.

Uh…what was that about?

She was the one who'd walked away…er, make that *drove* away…from him. After what he'd thought was a spectacular weekend. Without even telling him goodbye. She'd made it pretty clear she was obviously not *that* interested in him. She hadn't even given him her number.

Yeah, he probably could have gotten it from Brody. But then he'd have to admit that he'd felt something more for her than he was willing to consider. Even though he'd liked her from pretty much the first minute he'd met her.

She made him laugh. And something about her

made him feel like he could be himself around her. And not the grumpy cowboy his brothers were always accusing him of being, but a better, kinder version of himself.

He'd fallen for her that weekend—fallen for her whip-smart sense of humor, her silly giggle, the kindness she'd shown her dog, the goofy way she'd bellyflopped into the water when he'd taken her swimming, and the soft kitten sighs she'd made when he'd pressed his lips to the deliciously smooth skin of her inner thigh. Which meant that it was probably a good thing she *had* driven away from him without giving him her number. Because she was too good for a guy like him, too sweet, too tender-hearted. He would have only hurt her in the end when he took off running. Which he would do. Because that's what he always did. Leave before giving anyone a chance to leave him first.

He swallowed as he looked at Elizabeth, all the memories of their weekend now flooding his senses. Memories of her naked and straddling his waist in the bed of his truck, of waking up naked and wrapped around each other, of her naked except for a pair of strappy silver sandals the night of the wedding. *Damn*. Why did so many of his memories of that weekend have to do with her being naked? And now he couldn't get the idea of getting her naked *again* out of his mind.

Bad idea, Lassiter.

Hadn't he just reminded himself of why she was too good for him? And how he was only going to hurt her?

Now the silence between them had stretched out too far.

He didn't know what to say.

Apparently, he didn't have to say anything, as a loud rumbling sound broke the silence.

She giggled again as she pressed her hand to her stomach. "Sorry. I haven't eaten all day. I was so excited to come up here, I didn't even think about food."

Ford smiled, thankful for the distraction. "Then we need to remedy that. How do you feel about barbeque?"

"If you're talking about pulled pork and a side of ribs, then I feel great about it."

He nodded. "A woman after my own heart. Have you been to the Tipsy Pig yet?"

She laughed. "No, but with a name like that, I feel like I need to go there immediately."

"I swear it's got the best barbeque in three counties. It's a cool little bar with a big outdoor patio and they play live music on most weekends. It's on the west side of town. You probably saw it when you drove through."

She shook her head. "I came straight here. I haven't been anywhere in Woodland Hills yet. I haven't even driven through town."

"Dang. Sounds like you need a tour of our fair city then. I'll be happy to drive you around. Although the whole tour will probably take all of ten minutes. We've only got five streets, one bank, two grocery stores, and four churches. We used to have a stoplight, but the city-council voted to take it down a couple years ago. But I can show you where to buy dog food, point out the hair salon, and tell you where to find the best burger and who has great soft-serve ice-cream."

"All things I need to know. But you didn't mention pizza. Please tell me I can get a pepperoni pizza in this five-street town."

"You won't get it delivered out here, but we do have a pizza joint. Although the best pizza is in Creedence, so you'll have to decide if it's worth the twenty-minute drive."

"In Denver, I drove twenty minutes just to get to work every day. I'd drive thirty for a great slice." She touched the bandage on her forehead. "Speaking of pizza, are you sure you don't want to just order something to go? I'm kind of a mess."

"We're not fancy around here," he told her, offering her a flirty grin. "And you look great to me."

He loved the little smile he caught that tugged at her lips before she turned away to call for Thor and Dixie. "Can you give me two minutes to pull myself together then we can go?"

"Sure. I'll let the dogs out." He whistled for the dogs to follow him, and they raced after him as he crossed the yard toward the barn. He'd seen a sheet of plywood leaning against it when he'd come out to grab her bag before. Carrying it back, he laid it in front of the door, covering the biggest holes in the porch. He'd come up with something better tomorrow, but for now, this would have to do.

Elizabeth nodded her agreement as she came out the front door. "This is great," she told him as she pulled the door shut behind her. She'd brushed out her hair and pulled some of her bangs over the bandage. She had her pink tote bag over her shoulder, and she held it up as she followed him to the truck. "I brought my notebook with me. I thought we could work on the supply list while we eat."

"Sure," he said as he held the truck door open for her and the dogs to get in.

"I'm trying not to get freaked out about it," she said, after he'd started the engine and pulled out of the driveway. "But I was thinking about how long the Johnsons had lived here and wondering how many other people might have keys to this place."

"Good point," he said, turning onto the main road. "Add new locks to the list, and I'll get them installed first thing tomorrow."

Elizabeth groaned as she took another bite of her pulled pork sandwich. "You were right," she told Ford. "This *is* amazing. And this view. Oh my gosh."

They were sitting on the patio next to the river and had already plowed through a basket of cheese curds and fried pickles before their sandwiches arrived.

Several people had waved to Ford as they'd walked through the bar area to the outside, and he and the waitress had called each other by name when she seated them and took their drink orders. Her name was Shana, and he'd introduced Elizabeth and said she'd just bought the old Johnson place.

"Oh, I know," Shana had said, giving her and

Ford a knowing grin. "I've already heard *all* about you. *And* you," she'd told Ford with a wink. *What did that mean?* Then, she'd turned back to Elizabeth with a genuine smile. "Welcome to Woodland Hills and the Tipsy Pig. I recommend the sangria-swirled frozen margarita."

Elizabeth had taken her up on her recommendation and was surprised to see she'd already downed half the delicious drink.

The night felt perfect. Sitting outside, drinking a wine-swirled margarita and enjoying conversation and great food with a handsome cowboy who kept bumping his knee against hers. What could be better?

Maybe if he were her *actual* boyfriend, instead of her fake one.

That fantasy had been fun for a hot minute, but now they were getting back to reality as they talked through the order of repairs to the farmhouse and made a list of supplies they planned to get at the hardware store tomorrow.

Ford had just given her the name of an electrician he trusted when a tall dark-haired guy wearing a cowboy hat and a faded red T-shirt that stretched across his muscular chest walked up behind him and knocked Ford's hat off his head. "Think fast, bro."

Elizabeth braced for Ford to push back his chair and face-off with the guy, but instead he just righted his hat as the guy slumped down in the chair between them and stole a fry off Ford's plate.

Then he leaned back in his chair and grinned at Elizabeth as if he were the Cheshire cat who had just cunningly swallowed a canary. "So, you're the girl who finally stole Ford's cold, broken heart, huh?"

She tried to keep her features even as she glanced at Ford. *Cold, broken heart?* What did that mean? And who was this guy? A friend of Chad's? Did they need to keep up the ruse of her being Ford's girlfriend?

She tried for a casual shrug. "Yep. That's me."

Ford raised an eyebrow at her and completely ignored the fact that the guy had now picked up the second half of his sandwich and taken a bite of it. "Chevy, this is Elizabeth. Elizabeth, this is my brother, Chevy."

Ohhh. This made much more sense now. When the guy had called Ford 'bro', he really meant his 'bro'.

She opened her mouth to respond but didn't get a chance as Chevy slapped the table then let out a laugh. "No way. *This* is Elizabeth? *The* Elizabeth? The one from Brody's wedding who you haven't shut up about for the last month?" He pushed his hat back and grinned even wider at her. "Nice to meet you, darlin'."

Ford punched his brother's shoulder. "Seriously? Would you shut up?"

"What? I can see now why you're so smitten." He winked at Elizabeth. "Although I hadn't realized you two were so serious. I had to hear it from that putz, Duchette, that you were so serious you were moving in together."

Ford frowned. "When did you talk to Chad?"

Chevy jerked a thumb over his shoulder. "Just now. He's sitting at the bar telling everyone how you stole his contractor job and that you're moving off the ranch and into the old Johnson's place with your girlfriend, some chick from the city." He tipped his hat to Elizabeth. "No offense intended. His words, not mine."

"None taken," she replied. She was still stunned by the fact that he knew who she was and by his comments about how Ford hadn't stopped talking about her for the last month.

Then his last words sank in.

Oh. No. Chad was inside the restaurant. And he was telling everyone that she and Ford were an item. She didn't know what to do. Should she play along, or would Ford laugh it off as he filled his brother in on the ruse?

She held her breath, waiting to see what Ford would do, then let it out in a rush as he reached across the table and picked up her hand.

"It's true," Ford said, his voice a little louder than before, and she suddenly realized that the couple from the next table over and the woman on her computer by the firepit had all stopped what they were doing and were possibly listening to their conversation.

Elizabeth squeezed his hand and tensed as she waited to hear Chevy's response. Would he see right through his brother's lie and out them while he stole another fry?

Chevy popped the French fry in his mouth and grinned at Ford. "Awesome. I call your room," he said, like they were teenagers and Ford was headed off to college.

Ford started to protest then eased back in his chair. "Fine with me. But it's gonna take us a few weeks to get the old farm in good enough shape to live in."

"Cool," Chevy said, then turned back to Elizabeth. "So, I guess you'll be staying at the ranch with us until then. Have you met Gramps yet?"

Elizabeth shook her head at his comment about staying at the ranch, but he must have thought she was responding to having met their grandfather.

"Well, don't let the old coot talk you into playing poker with him. Especially for money. He acts innocent, but the man's a card shark. I swear he cheats." He pushed up from the chair and nudged his brother's shoulder. "I'm adding a beer to your tab. See you guys at home later."

Then he ambled back inside the restaurant, leaving Elizabeth staring after him trying not to let her mouth hang open.

Ford squeezed her hand again. "You ready to get out of here?"

She nodded. "Sure."

He glanced around the patio then lowered his voice. "We should probably get back to the ranch before someone calls my grandpa."

Elizabeth slugged back the last of her margarita then pushed back from her chair. Ford pulled her into his arms as she stood up, then leaned in to nuzzle her neck.

Her eyes fluttered closed at the sensation of his warm breath on her skin, and she sank into him.

Then reality hit her like an unexpected wave at the beach toppling her into the surf as he whispered,

"If Chad's inside running his mouth about us, we'd better make this story convincing." Then, as if another wave picked her up, the fantasy rolled back in as Ford tilted his head and captured her mouth in a kiss.

CHAPTER EIGHT

ELIZABETH MELTED INTO him, her arms going around Ford's neck, as her margarita-infused brain forgot to remind her that this was all for show.

His brain must have forgotten too, because he deepened the kiss, pulling her tighter against him and gripping her hip in his palm.

"Get a room," someone called out, bringing them both crashing back to reality as they split apart.

Elizabeth tried to catch her breath as she focused on collecting her notebook and pen and stuffing them back into her tote bag. *Holy hot cowboy.* She might be his fake girlfriend, but that kiss was all kinds of toe-curling real.

Ford put his arm around her again, and she kept her eyes forward, not wanting another run-in with Chad, as they walked through the restaurant and out the front door.

"That'll give 'em something to think about," he said when they'd made it back to the truck.

Them. *And* her.

It had taken some convincing on his part, but Ford finally talked Elizabeth into spending the night at their ranch. There was no way he was letting her sleep on an air mattress in that house alone. He wasn't sure when he'd turned into such a nervous Nellie, but his protective side seemed to come out when Elizabeth was involved.

She'd tried to argue, telling him she didn't want to impose, and that she'd be fine, but he swayed her with an argument involving more spiders and the reminder that they didn't know who had keys to the old farmhouse.

He hadn't seen any signs, so he didn't really think she had one, but he used the fact that she might have a concussion and shouldn't be alone to shoot down her arguments about staying in a hotel.

But now, as they drove up to the ranch, he was suddenly rethinking his idea. Maybe he should have let her stay in a hotel, and just convinced her to let him sleep in the chair at the foot of her bed. If her introduction to Chevy had been any indication of how this was going to go, Ford prayed the house would be empty. He hoped to get her settled before Gramps and his other brother, Dodge, took at crack at razzing him in front of her.

No such luck. This was not the night his prayers were answered. Both his youngest brother and his grandfather's pickups were in front of the house when they pulled up.

"Wow, this place is gorgeous," Elizabeth said as they got out of the truck. She held Thor in her arms as she looked around the ranch.

He'd lived here since he was a boy, and he loved

the place, but now he looked around with her, imagining it as if he were seeing it for the first time.

The large rambling two-story farmhouse sat nestled against the mountains behind it. The stone and wood exterior with huge windows looking out over the ranch gave it a cabin-type feel. A long porch ran the length of the front where Gramps and Gran used to sit together in matching rocking chairs. They'd added several chairs with more comfortable cushions over the years, and his grandfather had dispensed hours of wisdom, advice, and an occasional admonishment to all three boys while sitting on that porch.

The sun had set behind the mountain, giving the ranch an ethereal glow in the fading twilight, and the low moo of a cow floated through the warm summer night air.

A huge white barn with the Lassiter brand painted on the front sat across from the house. Corrals extended off either side, and several of their horses stood inside, one of them letting out a whinny as if welcoming Ford home. White fences ran along both sides of the driveway, enclosing green pastures, and several hundred head of cattle could be seen dotting the grassland leading up into the mountainside beyond the house.

A chicken coop and his grandmother's vegetable garden sat off to the right of the house. Although she'd been gone for five years now, his grandfather still kept up her patch of zucchini, squash, tomatoes, peas, green beans, and a little corn.

The ranch was well-taken care of, all of them taking pride in and working hard to maintain its upkeep. This place, and his grandparents, had taken in three boys that no one had wanted, and raised them to be the kind of men who would hopefully make their grandmother proud.

Elizabeth squealed in delight, and Thor squirmed in her arms as a handful of kittens came out from under the porch and ran toward them. Dixie, who was used to them, stretched out in the grass and let them tumble over her.

"You buried the lead, Ford." She bent down to let Thor free, then scooped a fluffy white and yellow kitten into her arms. "It would have taken a whole lot less convincing me to stay here if you'd told me you had *kittens*." She nuzzled the furrball under her chin then let it back down to play with its siblings.

Dropping the tailgate, he laughed as he unloaded her suitcase, an overnight bag, and a large duffel. It wasn't going to take much else to convince his family she was moving in with them for a few days.

"Maybe we should talk about the sleeping situation," he said as he slung the duffel over his shoulder, tucked the bag under his arm and wheeled the suitcase behind him toward the porch. "I'm putting your stuff in my room, but no one's going to believe you're my girlfriend if I've got you in my bed and I'm bunking on the couch. But don't worry. I'll give you the bed, and I'm happy to sleep on the floor." He opened the front door then stood back to let her go in ahead of him.

Which was his first mistake. He should have run recon before just letting her walk into the Lassiter lodgings.

He heard her soft intake of breath then almost

ran into her as she stopped just inside the doorway. Peering around her shoulder, he saw his grandfather standing in the kitchen, using a spatula to scrape cookies off a sheet pan and onto a cooling rack. And by the delicious butterscotch scent wafting through the house, they had to be his famous Oatmeal Scotchies.

The large living area was separated by a huge kitchen island with an oak dining room table on one side of the kitchen and a family room on the other. An enormous stone fireplace rose from the floor to the vaulted ceiling, and a large man-sized sofa faced it with two overstuffed recliners flanking its either side.

He assumed Elizabeth's gasp was not for his rugged cookie-baking grandfather but for his youngest brother, Dodge, who had just walked into the living room. Fresh out of the shower, barefoot and shirtless, with his hair still wet and one of his paperback spy novels tucked under his arm. He looked up from his phone, and grinned first at Elizabeth, then at Ford.

"Well, I'll be damned," he said. "Chevy just texted me that you'd be bringing an honest-to-goodness actual girl home with you, but I bet him a ten-spot he was lying."

CHAPTER NINE

OVER HER INITIAL shock of seeing a half-naked guy, who looked like a cross between the Marlboro Man and the cover model on her latest cowboy romance, walk into the room, Elizabeth let out her breath and tried to enjoy the show of Ford interacting with his family.

"Sorry, brother." The man, whom Elizabeth assumed had to be Dodge, dropped the book and his phone on the kitchen counter and offered to help Ford with her bags.

"I got it," Ford said. "Elizabeth, I'd like you to meet my grandfather, Duke Lassiter. And this idiot is my youngest brother, Dodge."

"Nice to meet you, Darlin'," Duke said, setting the cookie sheet down to come around the counter. "I made cookies just in case you showed up."

"You make cookies just in case the sun comes up," Dodge teased him.

Duke was tall like the boys, but a little rounder in the middle—maybe due to all the homemade cookies. He had thick white hair, a handle-bar mustache, and with his hearty laugh seemed to Elizabeth like a cross between Sam Elliott and Santa

Claus. He waved off her handshake and engulfed her in bear hug, wrapping her in the scents of leather, Old Spice, and butterscotch. "We're happy to have you, Elizabeth. Our home is your home."

Wow. They were all being so nice to her.

Dodge opened his arms to give her a hug too, but Ford shoved her duffel bag into his chest. "You can hug her after you've put a shirt on."

The screen door banged, and Chevy rushed in. "Dang. I wanted to see you all's faces when she walked in the door. I told you it was her." He flashed her a smile, his teeth so white against his tan skin, that he could have been the star in a toothpaste commercial. "Hey, Elizabeth," he drawled.

"Hey Chevy," she said, unable to keep from smiling back.

He glanced into the kitchen then wrapped an arm around his grandfather's shoulder. "Yes. I was hoping you'd make cookies." Reaching over the counter, he grabbed a couple from the cooling rack and passed one to her before shoving the other one into his mouth. He groaned in pleasure as he chewed. "You haven't lived until you've tasted Gramps' Oatmeal Scotchies."

Her mouth had been watering ever since she'd walked into the vanilla and butterscotch scented house, and she groaned almost as loudly as Chevy had as she filled her mouth with the warm, chewy cookie. Then she pressed her lips together as she tried, and failed, to hold in a nervous giggle.

"It's okay," Dodge told her as he came back into the room, this time wearing a white T-shirt with Ford tight on his heels. "We all sounded like that when we first tried them." He picked up a cookie, stuffed it in his mouth and then closed his eyes in bliss and let out an exaggerated groan. "So good."

"Can I get you something to drink?" Duke asked her. "Glass of water? Coffee? Cup of hot tea? Shot of whiskey?"

She laughed. "Sure. Water. Not the whiskey. I mean, some water would be nice."

All of them converged on the kitchen, as if it took four grown men to get her a glass of water. They joked and razzed each other as Dodge dropped ice cubes into glasses then passed them to Ford to fill with water. Duke stacked warm cookies on a plate, and Chevy grabbed a stack of napkins. Each of them also took a turn wrestling with or ruffling the neck of Thor, who was racing around, gobbling up the attention and hoping for a cookie to fall on the floor.

Even though she felt a little like Goldilocks, who had just stepped into the home of four burly, and way too handsome, bears, she couldn't help but like all these men. It was true, Ford's brothers were giving him a hard time, but it felt like it was all in good fun, and in no way malicious.

Ford pulled a chair out for her as his brothers and grandfather brought in the cookies and glasses and sat down around the table.

"So, Elizabeth," Duke said as he pushed the plate of cookies toward her. "Tell us about yourself."

Ford growled in the back of his throat. "You all are *not* giving her the third degree."

"What?" Duke asked, a look of pure innocence on his face. "I just want to get to know the girl. And to find out more about her than just what you've told us the last several weeks."

Heat rose to Elizabeth's cheeks, and her stomach did a little flip at the thought of Ford talking about her to his family.

She rested a hand on Ford's arm. "I don't mind," she told him, then turned back to his family. "There's not much to tell though. I'm pretty boring. I've never lived anywhere exciting. In fact, I've spent my whole life either living with or within ten minutes of my parents. I have a boring job as a CPA with a boring bachelor's degree in accounting."

Chevy propped his elbows on the table and dropped his chin into his hands like he was a little kid. "There has to be more. Because our brother seems to think you're fascinating."

Ford kicked him under the table.

She barked out a laugh then clapped her hand over her mouth. "The most fascinating thing I've ever done was a little over a month ago when I walked into a realtor's office and put an offer on a farmhouse in the mountains without ever having stepped foot on the property."

"No way," Dodge said.

"The pictures the realtor was showing her were of what the house looked like when the Johnson's still lived there," Ford told them.

Chevy's eyes widened. "Aww hell. You mean you didn't know it was a fixer-upper?"

"I think 'fixer-upper' is putting it kindly," Duke said with genuine concern in his voice. "Is it too late to get out of the contract? Surely there's some kind of law against that."

"I don't want to get out of the contract," she told them. "I mean, I was a little, well a lot, shocked at first. And I'll admit, I was trying not to cry when I pulled up and saw the white picket fence was just broken gray slats lying in a weed-filled yard. And I was just starting to think I'd made the biggest mistake of my life when your brother showed up. Then we walked through the house together, and he showed me the charm and the possibility of the place, and now I love it and can't wait to roll up my sleeves and start slapping up some shiplap."

"Hold on now," Ford said. "Nobody said anything about shiplap."

"It seems like every farmhouse worth its salt has some shiplap in it somewhere," she said, teasing him. To be honest, she wasn't sure if she even knew exactly what shiplap was. But they talked about it a lot on the fixer upper shows she watched.

"You all seem like you've got your work cut out for you with that place," Dodge said.

"Yeah, but it'll be kind of fun, too," Ford told them. "I always thought it was such a neat old house. It will be cool having a chance to restore some of it. And Elizabeth's already got some great ideas for updating the kitchen."

"And Ford has a great idea for updating the master bedroom," she added. Then dropped her gaze to the table to focus on the cookie crumbs in front of her instead of the teasing looks his brothers were giving to Ford. Maybe it was the mention of the bedroom, but the day suddenly caught up to her and she raised her hand to her mouth to stifle a yawn.

She hadn't hidden it from Ford though.

He pushed back his chair and stood. "This has been fun and all, but Elizabeth's had a heck of a day, and we should probably get to bed."

Oh. Wait. A second ago, she *had* been tired, but now, the thought of spending the whole night in the same room with Ford, even if he *had* offered to sleep on the floor, had blood surging through her veins and memories of the hot cowboy's naked body streaming through her brain.

Nope. Nobody said anything about getting naked, she reminded herself.

But she had just enough sangria-swirled margarita left in her to imagine what might happen if she accidentally fell on top of him in the middle of the night.

He took her hand and led her down the hallway to the last room on the left. Curious to see what his bedroom looked like, she was pleased to see that his bed was neatly made with a navy-blue comforter, and he had stacks of books on a tall bookshelf next to a small desk tucked into the corner of the room.

Dixie and Thor had padded down the hall after them and jumped up to sprawl out in the middle of the bed.

"Bathrooms through there," he said, pointing to a door at the back of the room. "I'll take the dogs outside and give you a chance to get settled."

She brushed her teeth and wished she had packed some other pajamas besides the shorty-shorts and thin tank top that she'd stuffed in her bag. She finished her bedtime routine and was reading a book as she sat up against the pillows—which she had totally breathed in and swooned over the scent of his cologne—by the time he came back in the room.

The dogs jumped up on the bed with her, and he handed her a glass of water and dropped two ibuprofens in her hand. "For your head," he said. "Anti-inflammatory. And they'll help with the pain if your knee acts up in the night."

This man. Protective, sweet, *and* thoughtful.

Why were they only *pretending* to be a couple when she should be dragging him into this bed with her right now?

She knew they had chemistry. They'd been great in bed together. Or he'd been great, at least. She had no idea how she was. But he had seemed to enjoy himself.

Oh yeah. Because he wasn't interested in a relationship, *or her*. She'd heard it with her own ears that he'd thought he was getting with someone else that weekend. Someone who was only looking for a good time and no commitment—just like him.

And it would be way too easy for her to fall head over heels in love with Ford Lassiter. Ha—like she wasn't halfway there already. But then, he'd walk away from her—he'd already told her that was what he did—and she'd be left with a broken heart and living right next door to the guy who'd shattered it.

And also, she'd just poured most of her life savings into a dilapidated farmhouse that would take all of her energy and probably what remained of her savings in the next few months.

All good reasons to keep things in the friend zone.
Good. It's settled then.

So why was she pulling down one side of the

covers and scootching over as she told him, "You don't have to sleep on the floor."

CHAPTER TEN

ELIZABETH SWALLOWED, HER heart pounding hard enough that she was surprised he couldn't hear it thumping against her chest. "I mean, this bed is plenty big enough for the two of us."

He narrowed his eyes as he studied her face. As if trying to decipher the true meaning behind her invitation. Her neck started to heat the longer he stared at her.

"It's just that we do have a big day ahead of us tomorrow," she said, trying to sound way more casual than she actually felt. "No use starting out with a sore back from sleeping on the floor."

He didn't say anything, just made one of those growling sounds in his throat as he took off his T-shirt and shimmied out of his jeans. Her mouth went dry at the sight of his strong muscular back and the way his biceps flexed as he shucked out of his jeans. The whisper of his zipper had heat surging through her veins as the sound brought back memories of the last night they'd spent together. He turned and she tried not to stare at his rock-hard abs or the V-shaped dips that slid under the waistband of his snug black boxer briefs.

She wiggled down under the covers on her side, all too aware of how close his body was to hers as he slid into the bed next to her.

He snapped off the bedside light. "You need anything else?" he asked quietly.

Yes. You.

"No, I'm good," she said just as softly.

"Good night then." He rolled onto his side, facing away from her.

"Good night. See you in the morning." She rolled onto her side too, but facing him.

Just enough moonlight shone in through the window to see the outline of his bare shoulder. She reached up, holding her hand just above his arm, her palm practically sizzling with the energy coursing between them.

Then Dixie, who had been sprawled next to Thor at the bottom of the bed, climbed over her legs, stretching out her body as she settled herself between them.

Elizabeth's hand dropped, and she buried it into the dog's silky fur.

Friend zone it is then.

At least for tonight.

Ford woke up the next morning with his body wrapped around Elizabeth's and his palm firmly cupping one of her breasts.

He closed his eyes again, relishing the feel of her lush body snuggled against his. She fit perfectly. He let out a breath and opened his eyes, trapped between wanting to stay in that dream-state with her and needing to look at her. He gazed down at her creamy skin, the curve of her neck, the rosebud pink of her supple lips. Everything in him wanted to lean in and nuzzle her neck, kiss her sweet mouth.

Hell, he wanted to do more than that. He wanted to ravage her. For hours.

He knew his feelings for her were true, because as much as he wanted to ravage her, he was also content to just lay here and hold her in his arms. It would be really easy to get used to waking up next to this gorgeous woman every day.

And it would be really easy to break her heart when he got scared and walked away. Or on the flip side, it would break him if she suddenly realized she could do better than a surly cowboy like him, and she decided to leave.

Neither situation was one he was willing to risk happening.

Which is why he needed to get *out* of this bed and *into* a cold shower. Besides, he had cattle to feed and chores to do. He was sure his brothers were probably already up, and he was still lying in bed fantasizing about a woman he never could, or should, have.

He gently tried to pull his hand away, then tried not to moan as his palm skimmed over the thin fabric of her tank top and grazed her taut nipple. She sighed in her sleep and snuggled closer, her hand covering his and holding it tighter against her breast.

Maybe he could stay in bed a little longer.

Elizabeth rolled over twenty minutes later to find the bed empty. Well, empty of the hot cowboy she'd been dreaming about and had possibly been cuddling with. Had she dreamed it, or had he really been holding her boob? She could almost still feel his large hand cupping her breast. *Sigh.* He was gone now though. But there was still a hundred-pound golden retriever and a tiny Havanese curled in bed with her.

She rubbed bellies and scratched ears for a few minutes, then she staggered into the bathroom and groaned at the sight of herself in the mirror. Besides the bandage clinging to her forehead, her hair was sticking up in several places and the strands around her temples had curled into such crazy wings, she looked like she might be able to take flight. Her mascara was smudged under her eyes, and the pillowcase had left a wrinkle mark across her cheek.

Ugh. Maybe it was a *good* thing Ford hadn't woken up next to her, she thought as she stripped out of her pajamas and stepped into the shower.

Thirty minutes later, with clean clothes, moisturized skin, and a swipe of mascara, she felt more like herself as she exited the bathroom and stuffed her things back into her bags. She had no idea if she'd be back here tonight or not.

She did know this was her chance to get to know a little bit more about the man she'd been fantasizing about for weeks. Skimming her fingers over the books on his shelves, she tilted her head to read the titles. Several old Louis L'Amour westerns, a tattered copy of *Lonesome Dove*, a few of the older John Grisham legal thrillers, a couple of Stephen

King's books…that was kind of interesting…and various editions of the Farmer's Almanac. The next shelf held some reference books like *Storey's Guide to Raising Beef Cattle*, *The Cattle Health Handbook*, and a number of others on farming and ranching. She loved that Ford liked to read.

His bookshelves held a few knickknacks, an old baseball with a smudged signature, and a couple of framed photos, one of him and his brothers, all grinning like fools as they held up different sized fish, with a lake in the background. They looked to be in late grade school, maybe junior high, but it was obvious from their hair, Chevy's dark mop, Dodge's white-blond head, and Ford's dirty blond one, who was who. There was also one of just Ford, wearing a green cap and gown and holding a degree certificate from Colorado State University, with his arms around Duke and a woman Elizabeth supposed was his grandmother. They all looked so proud.

She wandered over to Ford's desk, just glancing at what was on top, not ready to start pulling open drawers and full-on snooping. The desktop was fairly tidy, a few folders marked with ranch and cattle topics, post-it notes, a pen from the local bank, and a souvenir drink glass full of loose change.

She liked having these little glimpses into who Ford Lassiter was. To know what he liked to read, that his family and this ranch were important to him. He didn't talk much about himself, but she knew from the time they'd spent together that he had a protective streak that probably came from being the oldest brother of three.

Rummaging through her bags, she found her

sneakers and some socks and finished getting ready. Then she eased open the bedroom door and slipped into the hallway. But there was no reason to be quiet. The house was empty, except for her and the dogs. There was a note on the counter telling her to help herself to coffee and that there was a plate of scrambled eggs and biscuits and gravy still warm in the oven for her.

Wow. Was this the way these guys ate every morning?

She dug into the fluffy eggs and shoveled thick sausage gravy into her mouth. She'd just finished her plate and a second cup of coffee when Ford came inside.

"Mornin'," he said. "You get enough to eat? I could make you a couple more eggs…"

She pressed her hands to her stomach. "Oh my gosh, no. I ate too much as it is."

"I just finished my morning chores, and the hardware store opens in ten minutes. You ready to get started?"

"Yes," she said, pushing up out of her chair. "I can't wait."

Although, as it turned out, she could wait. Because they had such a big order, it took them a while to compile all the lumber and supplies they needed. Ford had pulled his truck around the back, and she'd gone on a coffee run while they were loading it.

It was fun for her to sit on a bench outside the hardware store and observe the town. Woodland Hills was laid out in a square, with a common area in the center, holding the city courthouse and a large grassy area, complete with a gazebo where Ford had told her they hosted weddings, town meetings, and occasionally had bands play in the summer.

Businesses lined the four main streets facing the courthouse, with the bank on one corner and the main grocery store on the other. The town had a true mountain feel to it, with most businesses trimmed in cedar and bearing dark green awnings over their front doors and windows. Big cedar pots filled with white alyssum and trumpet flowers spilling over their sides sat on the sidewalks next to old-fashioned streetlamps, and several businesses had a dog bowl full of fresh water sitting outside their front doors.

On her trek to the adorable little coffee shop up the street, she passed an insurance agency, the hair salon that Ford had pointed out the night before, and a fun little shop that seemed to carry all sorts of pet accessories, from pet food to leashes and collars, to cat trees, and bird cages. She'd even seen a few cute doggy outfits in the window. She mentally marked it as a place she wanted to come back to.

When Ford still hadn't come out after a few minutes, she pulled her latest book, *Remarkably Bright Creatures* by Shelby Van Pelt, out of her tote bag and figured she'd read a few pages while she waited.

She was deep in the world of the Sowell Bay Aquarium when a shadow fell across the pages, and she stopped reading to look up.

A woman about her age, with blond hair and large round glasses was standing next to her and reading over her shoulder. "Great book. I love this part."

Elizabeth smiled up at her. "I'm really enjoying it.

I never thought I'd fall in love with a curmudgeonly octopus, but Marcellus has stolen my heart."

The other woman laughed and gestured to the empty spot on the bench next to her. "May I?"

"Of course," she said, pulling her tote bag closer to give the woman a place to sit. Thor popped his head out of the bag and made a frenzied attempt to lick the newcomer's face.

"Oh my gosh, how adorable," she said, scrubbing Thor's ears and blissfully accepting the puppy-kisses to her chin. "I'm Maisie Graham, one of the local librarians. Hence the awkward book conversation." She shrugged. "And also, the blatant use of the word 'hence'."

Elizabeth laughed with her. "I'm Elizabeth. Cole. And this is Thor. I just bought the Johnson place, and we're fixing it up." She jerked a thumb over her shoulder to the front door of the shop. "Hence why I'm sitting on this bench reading a book while I wait for a truckload of supplies that cost more than a used car to be loaded up for me."

Maisie wrinkled her small nose. It had a spray of freckles across it and was pink as if recently sunburned. "I have to admit, I actually knew who you were. Woodland Hills is a small town. We already had a forum last night where we flashed your picture and most of your life story on the side of the courthouse in a twenty-minute PowerPoint presentation."

Elizabeth blinked at the other woman. "Are you serious?" she breathed out.

Maisie laughed and nudged her shoulder. "No. I'm teasing you. But that's what living here sometimes feels like. Everyone knows everyone and gossip flows faster than a mountain stream after a heavy snow run off."

She wasn't exactly sure what that meant, but she got the general picture. And was thankful that the PowerPoint thing had been a joke.

"How are the renovations going?" Maisie asked.

"We're just getting started today," Elizabeth told her. "To be honest, I'm a little overwhelmed. I thought I had a handle on it, but then when I saw all the things we just added to the cart in the hardware store, I'm not sure. Thankfully, I've been thinking about paint colors and kitchen ideas for weeks now, so at least I'd already made some of those decisions. But it feels like there are a million more to make."

"I remember. I bought a little cottage just off downtown and spent a year remodeling the interior. It's a lot, but's it's worth it."

"Did you use a contractor?" Elizabeth asked her, praying she didn't say she'd used Chad Douche-Canoe.

Maisie shook her head. "Nope. Just me. I watched a lot of HGTV and How-To You Tube videos."

"Wow. I'm impressed."

"I was quite impressed with myself, actually. I never thought I could install vinyl plank flooring or tile a bathroom, but I figured it out, and I love my little house. I've got a bunch of home improvement books and magazines I could loan you, if you want some more ideas."

"Yes, I would love that. But I don't want to put you out."

"You're not. I'm offering. And this is what I do. I'm a librarian. I matchmake people with books."

Ford came out of the hardware store and strode over to their bench. Elizabeth handed him his coffee as he tipped his hat at her new friend. "Hey Maisie."

"Hey Ford. How's your summer?"

"We've had some rain and the crops look good, so I can't complain. How's the new bookmobile program working out?"

"Bookmobile?" Elizabeth asked.

Ford nodded as he took a sip of his coffee. "Maisie fixed up a little camper to be a bookmobile, and she drives it around to the more rural areas, so kids can still have access to books in the summer."

"Wow. How neat," Elizabeth said, even more impressed with the other woman.

Maisie shrugged. "I'm having fun with it. You know how I love to share books. I just offered to bring Elizabeth some home improvement books."

"That would be great," he told her. "She must have told you she bought the old Johnson farm. We'll be out there working all day if you want to stop by."

Elizabeth felt a twinge of jealousy over the familiar ease that these two had with each other. But it disappeared as Ford rested a hand on her shoulder and at the hopeful way Maisie asked if Dodge was going to be there.

"I'm not sure. He's supposed to be tracking down a sander for the floors today, so hopefully he'll show up at some point," Ford said.

"Oh. Okay. Well, I'll try to drop by then," Maisie said a little too quickly. "I mean, with the home improvement books, of course."

"You're welcome any time," Ford told her.

"Great to meet you," Elizabeth told her, hoping she really had just met a new friend.

"Yes, you too," Maisie said, pushing her glasses up her nose as she stood. "See you soon."

"We went to school with Maisie," Ford explained. "She was in Dodge's class, but we've known her since we were kids. Her family's farm isn't too far from ours."

That explained the casual ease of their conversation. "I like her," Elizabeth said, dumping her empty coffee cup in the trash can in front of the store.

Ford had downed his in a few gulps, and he tossed his cup in after hers then took her hand as they walked to the truck. He'd held it several times when they were in the hardware store too—at least whenever anyone else was around. He was pretty committed to making the town believe they were together. He'd casually put his arm around as they'd studied cabinet door handles. He'd even dropped a kiss on her neck while they'd waited in line at the register. If anyone saw them together, they would seem to be a real couple.

The only problem was that Elizabeth was starting to believe it herself.

CHAPTER ELEVEN

ELIZABETH SIGHED AS Ford pulled up in front of the house.

"What's that big sigh for?" he asked.

"I was hoping it might look better today."

He nudged her shoulder. "You'll be surprised at how much a little spit and polish will do to this house. Just cleaning the windows will make it seem brighter in there, and once we start painting, it'll make a world of difference."

"I'll take your word for it." She let the dogs out then helped Ford unload the truck.

He set the last of the supplies on the kitchen counter then pulled out a black plastic box. "I bought you a present."

She stared at him as he placed the box in her hands. "For me? Why?"

"You'll see why. This little baby will become your best friend in the next few months."

The word 'DeWALT' was stamped in yellow on the top. She flipped the snaps on the side then opened the lid to reveal a cordless drill. She lifted it out and tested the weight of it in her hand. "Nice. But what do I do with it?"

Ford laughed. "*Everything.*" He reached back into the bag and pulled out another small box. "Here's a set of drill bits. And I got you an extra battery."

He showed her how to use it, how to switch out the bits, which button to push to get it to spin the opposite way, how the light came on when she started to drill, and how to switch out the battery. She tried to focus on his directions, but it was tough since her skin seemed to tingle every time their hands touched, or his body brushed against her.

"I think I got it," she said, holding up the drill at the end of his lesson. "I'm ready to screw something." Her eyes widened as she clapped her hand to her mouth. "I mean, drill something. Wait, no, I mean—"

He held up his hand, a flirty gleam in his eye. "I get the idea." He pushed the kitchen table up against the wall. "We can use this as command central. We'll keep the master lists and all our tools here. If we need something, we put it on the list. If we use something, we put it back. I'll set up a couple of chargers here too, then we'll always have a fresh battery when we need one. All my power tools are DeWALT too, so they use the same batteries. Sound good?"

She nodded, still embarrassed by her 'screw something' comment, but glad he'd moved on. Although she did love the way he said *power tools*.

"Great. I'll go get my tools, and we can get started." He headed for the door, then turned back to offer her a cocky grin. "And don't worry, I'm an expert when it comes to finding ways to screw and drill."

She barked out a laugh as he pushed through the door. "Good to know, Lassiter," she called after him.

When he came back in, they unloaded all the tools and set up their workstation. Elizabeth created another station by the sink in the kitchen for all the cleaning supplies. They talked through their plan of spending most of the day cleaning up, tearing down old wallpaper, and prepping for painting.

The morning flew by in a whirl of cleaning, sweeping, measuring, demo, and making more lists. Elizabeth had started in the kitchen, scrubbing down the cabinets in preparation for their fresh new coat of paint. There were only five upper cabinets, one on each side of the sink and two on either side of the oven. The fifth was a corner cabinet that connected both sides.

Ford showed her how to unscrew the hinges so they could take the cabinet faces off, and she was on her knees on the counter working on the one next to the sink. She pointed at the corner cabinet. "You know, I always hate that type of cupboard. You can't reach anything in the back, and stuff always gets lost as it gets shoved to the sides. What would you think about taking that one out and installing open shelving in this corner instead? I've got some pretty bowls and a couple of plants that I think would look neat displayed there."

Ford studied the space then nodded. "I think that's a great idea. And that means we have one less cabinet to paint. Sounds like a win-win."

"Yay." She raised her hands in a cheer, but the motion and her precarious perch on the edge of the counter, caused her to wobble. She toppled off the side, releasing something between a shriek and a grunt as she fell back.

Right into Ford's arms.

She clung to him and let out a shaky breath. "I've never felt so clumsy as I've been in this house. Thank goodness you're here." She tried not to think about how heavy she must be or if she was hurting his back, but instead, she let herself be captured in the deep gaze of his slate blue eyes. "Whenever I'm around you, I just keep falling…" The words hung in the air as she peered up at him, her hands clutching his broad shoulders.

His voice was gruff, but soft, as he whispered, "Then I'll just keep catching you." His gaze dropped to her mouth, and butterflies took off in her belly, swirling in a dizzy whirl of manic motion. Heat rose to her chest as he leaned in.

Her lips parted, anticipating the press of his mouth to hers. His grip tightened on her arms, pulling her closer to his chest. Her hand left his shoulder and slid up his neck and into the ends of his hair.

He leaned closer still, and she sucked in a breath, as if drawing his mouth nearer to hers. Slowly, his lips grazed hers, in the barest whisper of a kiss, and a soft sigh escaped her.

The sound must have shattered his control because he pressed his mouth to hers in a kiss filled with desire and hunger.

She met his passion, digging her fingers into his hair, clutching his bicep, as his tongue slipped between her lips.

He shifted her weight, setting her butt back on the

counter, and her legs automatically wrapped around his waist. His hands slid under her shirt and up her back. The feel of his big palms running over her skin sent heat coursing through her.

His tongue explored her mouth as his hands raked over her body, skimming the edges of her breasts, gripping the sides of her waist, digging his fingers into her hips as he pulled her tighter against him.

She gave it all back—urging more of his touch as she pressed into him. Kissing him with all the bottled-up passion she'd spent the last few weeks suppressing. She'd gone to bed every night for the last month thinking about—or trying *not* to think about—the feel of him, kissing her, touching her, the solid weight of his body on top of her.

Gripping the hem of her shirt, he pulled away just long enough to yank it over her head and toss it to the floor. He peered down at her as he filled his hands with her breasts, the hunger apparent in his expression then in his actions as he laid a trail of warm kisses along her neck and across her chest.

Her back arched as she offered more of herself to him—reveling in the scrape of his whiskered jaw against her tender skin. But she wanted more of him too. Wanted to feel his skin against hers. He must have felt the same because she only had to tug at the back of his T-shirt then he was pulling it off and chucking it on the floor with hers.

Another moan sounded as he pulled her against him—she wasn't sure if it was him or her this time—but she did know that all she wanted was to be naked and under this man.

His nimble fingers splayed across her back, and he had just released the clasp of her bra when they heard a horn honking as a truck came barreling down the driveway.

CHAPTER TWELVE

FORD GLANCED BEHIND him then pressed his forehead to Elizabeth's. "My brother has *the* worst timing."

"Your brother? Gah." She pushed him back so she could get off the counter but forgot that her bra had just been unfastened, and the motion had her straps falling down her arms and the girls threatening to break free.

She knew how they felt.

She wasn't done with Ford either.

Pressing her hand to her chest, she held her bra in place as she and Ford scrambled for their shirts. A truck door slammed, and Elizabeth grabbed her top and sprinted toward the bathroom. Chevy's voice called out at the same time she slammed the door shut behind her.

Ford was on his own. She'd only just met his brother the night before, she didn't think flashing him her goodies this morning would make a real great impression. Thank goodness they hadn't gone any further.

Wait. No. Not thank goodness. She wanted to weep from the ache of having had to stop. Thank goodness they hadn't been caught in an even more compromising position, like the one they'd been headed for.

She quickly reclasped her bra and pulled her shirt on. Thankfully, she caught a glimpse of herself in the mirror above the sink. *Holy crazy hair.* Dang. If only they'd had twenty more minutes, Ford could have really mussed up her hairdo. She smoothed her bangs but couldn't do anything to change the kiss-swollen plumpness of her lips.

Pasting on a smile that she hoped looked totally normal, and not like she'd been about to tear Ford's clothes off and beg him to take her against the counter—a nervous giggle escaped her at the thought she would *or could* do such a thing—she exited the bathroom.

And came to face to face with Chevy Lassiter, who was grinning at her like he knew every dirty thought in her head.

He dipped his chin. "Sorry 'Lizabeth, didn't mean to interrupt."

"Oh gosh, we were just working on taking the cabinet doors off," she said, her words coming out a little too breathy as she awkwardly pulled down the front of her shirt.

Chevy offered his brother—who was glaring at him with a look that could cause a thousand deaths—a knowing grin. "I just hate it when I try to take off a cabinet door, and my clothes fall off instead."

"All right," Ford said, avoiding Elizabeth's gaze. "You've had your fun. Now what are you doing here? Did you find a sander?"

"No, Dodge is working on that though. I found something better. I brought manpower." He motioned out the front window where a line of half a dozen vehicles were pulling down the driveway.

"Manpower?" Elizabeth asked.

"Heck, yeah. Ford told us how you got hurt yesterday falling through that rotted out porch, so there was no way we were gonna let that happen again. I called a couple of guys to come help me tear that old thing off and build you a new one."

She turned to Ford. "Did you know about this?"

He shrugged. "I knew we'd eventually have to fix it, so I got the lumber for it this morning. But I didn't know Chevy was going to bring ten guys to build it."

Elizabeth pointed to the three elderly ladies climbing out of a Buick. "Is that your muscle? They must build 'em different up here in the mountains."

Chevy laughed. "You're funny. I like that. But no, that's *your* muscle. Those three gals were Miss Ida's bridge partners, and they called in the women of the First Presbyterian church to come help you clean this place up."

Elizabeth pressed a hand to her chest as she watched the women pull mops and buckets and a vacuum cleaner out of the trunk of the big car. "Lord have mercy. Thank goodness *they* weren't the ones who pulled up first."

Chevy let out a loud laugh. "I was grabbing some coffee at the gas station this morning and ran into Ruby Foster, she's the tall thin one. I told her you'd just bought the place and that it was in worse shape than you'd imagined, but that you were starting to work on renovating it today. She was Ida's best friend, and she told me she wanted to help. She said she'd gather the troops and be here by noon."

Elizabeth glanced down at her watch, surprised to see it was already close to twelve. Where had the morning gone? "That's so nice. But I don't think I have the resources to pay all these people."

"Don't you even try to pay us," Ruby said as she and the other women pushed through the screen door. "We loved Frank and Ida, and it's our *honor* to help you create a new home out of theirs." She set down all the cleaning supplies and came to Elizabeth, picking up her hands and squeezing them. "This is what we do in Woodland Hills. We're here for each other. Now you just let us help and then someday when you see a neighbor in need, you step in to help them."

Elizabeth nodded as she fought back tears. "I will."

Ruby patted her hand. "Good. Now, I'm Ruby Foster, I live in the little blue house down the street from the bank. This is Greta Newton, she's the president of our local PEO chapter, and she lives in that big brick house across from the Lutheran church. And this is Mabel Turner. She and her husband have that farm out east of town, the one with the antique wagon out by the mailbox. Their oldest boy runs the butcher shop."

Elizabeth smiled, trying to keep up as she shook each woman's hand. "I'm so glad to meet you. I'm not sure where all those places are, or what PEO is, but I'm so glad to meet each of you."

Greta squeezed her hand and offered her a wink. "Oh, you will dear. PEO stands for Philanthropic

Education Organization. We help promote educational opportunities for women. We're all members, and we'll be inviting you to our next meeting. As soon as you're settled."

"They're a lovely bunch of women. And our treasurer makes the most delicious lemon bars you've ever tasted," Mabel told her. "It's worth coming to the meeting for those bars alone."

"Thank you so much. I was really close to my grandmothers, but I lost them both over the last several years. You all are making me feel like they're both here with me now."

Ruby smiled. "I'm sure they are, honey."

They were interrupted as Duke walked in, carrying a large box in his arms. The scent of barbecue sauce and smoked meat filled the air. "Somebody go grab the table and the rest of the food from the truck. I made enough pulled pork to feed an army."

"Yes, sir," both Ford and Chevy said as they headed out the door.

"Duke, oh my gosh, this is too much," Elizabeth said, clearing a place on the counter for the box of food.

"Nonsense," he said. "You're with Ford. And you're our new neighbor. We're practically family now."

She bit her bottom lip as she nodded, the stupid tears filling her eyes again. Ford must have caught sight of them as he walked back in carrying a folding table. He set the table against the wall and hurried over to her.

"Hey now," he said, wrapping an arm around her waist and pulling her away from the bustle of people filling the room and into the quiet of the mud room. "What's wrong?"

She swallowed back the emotion as she held tightly to his arm. "This is all just so nice. I can't believe all these people showed up here to help me." She lowered her voice to a whisper. "Although I think they mostly showed up for you. And for *us*. Which makes me feel guilty for accepting any of this. Because you know…"

There wasn't really an *us*. It was all an act.

She could tell he knew what she meant as he reached up and brushed at the wetness on her cheek. "Nobody's doing this for me, darlin'. I'm mostly a grumpy asshole who doesn't inspire kindness. They're doing this for *you*. You're their new neighbor *and* the most recent resident of Woodland Hills. Folks are neighborly here. This is just their way."

She wanted to believe him, but she still felt like they were deceiving all these nice people. "But what about Duke? He likes me because he thinks *you* like me."

Ford shook his head. "No. He likes you because you're you. Because you're funny and sweet and charming and smart. And because you complimented his Oatmeal Scotchies. Not because his grandson is sweet on you."

She swallowed again, caught up on his last words. Did he mean because *his grandpa* thought he was sweet on her, or because he *was* actually sweet on her?

This fake relationship thing was harder than it seemed. Especially for her, because too many of her feelings were far from fake. They might be pretending they were an actual couple, but the passion they'd just displayed on the kitchen counter was all too real.

She smiled up at him as she slipped her arms around his waist and hugged him. "I guess we'd better go get some pulled pork then."

He stopped her from pulling away, keeping one arm around her as he reached up to cup her cheek in his hand. "Hey, there'll be plenty of tears, and blood, and sweat, during this renovation, but don't waste tears on this part. This is *community*. And it's real."

Several *more* members of the community showed up that afternoon. They might have heard that Duke had made pulled pork, or they might have just wanted to help, but they all pitched in, and Elizabeth couldn't believe the difference they made in just a few hours.

Ida's friends and the women from the church wiped down walls, scrubbed the tile in the bathroom, and washed every window. They stripped wallpaper and cleaned the refrigerator and stove. Elizabeth had ordered a set of new stainless-steel appliances, but they wouldn't be delivered for several days, so she was glad to have use of the old ones. Thankfully she'd called ahead and gotten the water and electricity in the house turned on.

She and Ford finished taking down the cabinet faces and prepped the kitchen for painting. They had a steady stream of people going in and out of the back door, since Chevy and his crew had torn off the front porch. He and Ford had established that the footers and most of the joists were still in good condition, so the men were making great progress, and the whir of circular saws and the scent of sawdust filled the air.

Ford had arranged for a dumpster to be delivered that afternoon, but Elizabeth was happy to hear that some of the old wood and demo materials were being claimed for other projects or hauled away to be used as firewood.

Dodge had shown up with a sander, and he and Ford had just finished sanding and buffing the floors when Maisie walked in, her arms full of home improvement books.

She waved at Elizabeth. "Wow. This is amazing. I can't believe how much you've already gotten done."

"Yeah, I think half the town showed up," Elizabeth told her. She nodded to the stack of books. "Those look great."

But she wasn't sure the other woman was listening since Dodge had just ambled up to them.

He wore the standard Lassiter brother outfit of jeans, square-toed cowboy boots, T-shirts that seemed to hug their muscular chests with sleeves that stretched over muscled biceps, and either a cowboy hat or baseball cap.

Dodge took his cap off and swiped the back of his arm across his forehead, leaving his blond hair sticking up in damp tufts. His smile was shy as he ducked his head toward the librarian. "Hey Maisie. Good to see you."

"Yeah, you too. I…um…just stopped by to bring Elizabeth some books." She raised the books, but the motion toppled the stack and they fell from her hands.

Dodge grabbed them before they hit the floor and passed them back to her.

"Oh…gosh…thanks…but these are for her." She tried to pass the books to Elizabeth but fumbled them again.

Between the three of them, they caught the errant books and managed to get them into Elizabeth's hands.

"Are you here to help?" Dodge asked.

Maisie nodded eagerly. "Yeah, sure. What can I do?"

"We just finished sanding the floors upstairs, so I was going to sweep up the dust. You can help me with that if you want."

"Yes, I'd be glad to," she said, sounding as if he'd just invited her on a trip to Paris instead of to the second floor to do some vacuuming.

Elizabeth set the books on the counter. She was excited to look at them but had a feeling she'd be so tired by the time she left tonight, she'd probably be asleep before her head hit the pillow. Which made her wonder about where her pillow would be tonight. They had picked up new locks that morning, and after lunch, Ford had given Duke the task of installing them in the front and back doors.

Now that she didn't have to worry about some random person with a key letting themselves into her new house, she felt better about sleeping here. But she'd left all her stuff in Ford's room.

The thought of sleeping next to him again had her heart pounding, especially considering what had happened earlier in the kitchen. Would they get the chance to finish what they'd started? Just thinking about it had her body aching for his touch and her lips desperate for his kiss.

She looked across the room to where he was standing with his grandfather. She loved the way he listened to and showed such obvious respect and devotion to the older man. During the long night they'd spent watching the stars from the back of his pickup, Ford had shared with her how his mother had brought her three sons, all fathered—and abandoned—by different men, to live with her parents at Lassiter Ranch. She must have had a type—a deadbeat loser type. Although it seemed to Elizabeth that all three boys had turned into pretty great men.

Even though she'd only met him the night before, she gave Duke and his wife a lot of the credit for that. She could see how much he loved Ford and his brothers. She was sure it hadn't been easy to take on three rowdy boys who had all been rejected by their fathers and then left behind again when their mother took off as well.

Shame filled her heart knowing that she'd taken off on Ford too. Granted, they had only spent a few days together, but it had been a spectacular two days filled with laughter and conversation and mind-blowing sex. It had felt like they'd really had a connection, which made her feel even more guilty for just taking off and not even saying goodbye.

She *had* been embarrassed and humiliated, but Ford didn't deserve that. And she needed to tell him so. Except so far, they'd been too busy or distracted to talk about the weekend they'd shared. But this was a conversation they *needed* to have. She'd make sure it happened tonight.

Double squeals sounded from two women who had just walked in the back door, and Elizabeth held back a groan.

What are they doing here?

She recognized the two sisters, both a few years older than her, and both bullies. She'd been dealing with their condescension and snide remarks for years. It must have been just too easy to pick on the bigger girl with a smaller nickname.

A nickname she was trying to get away from. And one she didn't really want everyone in Woodland Hills to hear.

"Bitsy," they called out in unison, then made their way across the room to her, peering down at the oak flooring and around at the faded paint as if the house was covered in mold. They both wore short summer dresses, ankle boots, and carried designer purses over their arms. Their long, dark hair fell in perfect waves around their shoulders, and they probably spent more on cosmetics and hair products than Elizabeth had spent at the hardware store that morning.

Ford glanced up at her from across the room with a frown at the two women.

"My cousins," she mouthed. And that was all she had time to say before she was engulfed in hugs and waves of hairspray and expensive perfume.

"What are you guys doing here?" she asked when they finally let her go.

"We had to come," the older one said. "Your

mama told ours that you bought a farm, and we didn't believe it, so we had to see for ourselves."

"And a friend of mine told us you had a serious boyfriend who was one of the hottest bachelors in town," said the younger one. "We didn't believe that either."

"I told her she was lying. You haven't even had a boyfriend *at all* in the last five years."

"Let alone a ridiculously hot one," the younger sister chimed in.

"There you are, darlin'," Ford said, his voice extra slow and deep as he ambled around her cousins and swept her into his arms. He leaned down and captured her mouth in a kiss that was so hot, she was surprised steam didn't rise from their lips.

CHAPTER THIRTEEN

ELIZABETH WAS STILL dazed when Ford pulled away. He kept his arm around her, holding her close as he kept his gaze locked on hers.

His voice was low, but plenty loud enough for her cousins to hear. "It's killing me to have all these people around here when all I want to do is carry you off to my bed and spend the afternoon ruining your good reputation."

One of her cousins let out an audible gasp, and Ford turned to her while keeping one arm around Elizabeth's waist. "Sorry, I didn't see you all standing there."

Oh, I do like this man.

Elizabeth loved the shocked, and then miffed, looks on her cousin's faces. Apparently, they weren't used to *not* being noticed. And she knew they especially weren't used to having any attention given to *her* when they were around.

"Ford Lassiter, these are my cousins, Tracy and Regina. They live over in Creedence, but they drove all the way here to see me and my new house. Oh, and to meet you. Wasn't that nice?"

Ford cocked an eyebrow. "To meet *me*?"

"Yes. Apparently, they wanted to assure themselves you were real. And not a figment of my imagination. They simply couldn't *believe* that I have a boyfriend." She tilted her face up to his, and her lips curved into a coy grin. "And especially one as *ridiculously* handsome as you." He offered her a flirty grin in return, and she felt it all the way to her toes. She turned back to her cousins. "Although I've never made up a boyfriend before, so I'm not sure why anyone thinks I would now."

Ugh. Maybe she shouldn't have said that last part, because that was exactly what she had done. Everything with her and Ford was a figment of her imagination. Except for those crazy feelings she kept having. And that kiss he'd just given her. That felt pretty dang real.

Ford tilted his head and frowned at her cousins. "Why would you not believe Elizabeth had a boyfriend?"

"*Elizabeth?*" Tracy said with a laugh as she raised a perfectly manicured eyebrow in her direction. "Don't you mean *Bitsy*?" She said the nickname with the same disdain she'd used since they were kids.

Ford pulled her closer. "No. I mean Elizabeth. I don't really know anyone named Bitsy. I just know a smart, talented, funny, gorgeous woman named Elizabeth." His hand sat at her waist, and he ran his palm over her hip and gripped the side of it as he looked down at her and added an extra bit of that sexy drawl that made her knees go weak. "And I can't seem to keep my hands off her."

Her heart did a little flip as she blinked up at him. Did he really think those things about her? She'd always been a bookworm and smart. But she'd never had a man describe her as talented or funny. *Or* gorgeous. She didn't see herself that way either. But the conviction in Ford's words almost made her believe he thought they were true.

If she hadn't *already* fallen in love with him, she was pretty sure in that moment, she just tumbled right over the cliff.

Tracy puckered her lips like she just sucked on a lemon. "Are you being serious right now?"

Regina planted a hand on her hip and raised her nose toward Elizabeth. "Yeah, tell us the truth. You're really going out with *her*?"

Ford's grip on Elizabeth's hip tightened, and the muscles in his jaw twitched. "I don't think I like what you girls are implying."

"Neither do I," said Chevy, who came to stand on Elizabeth's other side, his voice and expression stern.

Both Tracy and Regina's eyes widened as they looked from one tall hot cowboy to the other.

"So, did you all come to help or just to insult my girlfriend?" Ford asked. "Because we could use an extra hand with pulling some weeds in the front yard."

"I'm sure we could find you some gloves," Chevy chimed in. "Wouldn't want to mess up those fancy manicures."

The expressions on the two sisters' faces looked as if Ford had just asked them if they wanted to shovel horse poop.

"No thank you," Tracy said, linking her arm

through her sister's. "I mean, we'd love to help, but we can't stay."

Regina nodded. "Yeah, we just popped in for a quick hello. But we've gotta run now."

Ford raised his chin to the back entrance. "Well, don't let the door hit you in the ass on the way out."

The two women hurried toward the mudroom, but Tracy stopped and offered Elizabeth a little wave before they left. "Bye Bitsy."

Elizabeth let out her breath as she heard the screen door shut behind them.

"Those two are a piece of work. I heard them talking smack about you when they got out of their car, so I followed them in," Chevy said. He touched Elizabeth shoulder. "You okay?"

"Yeah, I'm good," she told him. "Thanks for standing up for me."

"Of course. Even if you *weren't* with my brother, you don't deserve to be treated like that. You're sweet and funny and kind, and much prettier than either of those mean girls."

Chevy's praise had heat rising in her cheeks. "It's okay, Chevy. They're gone now. You don't have to say that stuff."

Chevy frowned and looked confused. "I don't care where those two heifers are, I wouldn't say it if I didn't mean it."

"It's true," Ford said. "And I don't want to insult your family, but I'm not real fond of your cousins. It seems like they only came here to put you down."

"They did," she said. "But it's nothing I'm not used to. They've been treating me that way since we were kids."

"Why did she call you Bitsy?" Chevy asked.

"It's a nickname that my little brother started. My parents originally called me Betsy, but he pronounced it *Bitsy*, and the whole family thought it was so cute that it stuck. And it somehow followed me all the way through school. No matter how many times I tried to get people to call me Elizabeth, they always came back to Bitsy. And not always in a kind way."

Chevy nodded. "If anyone knows about getting made fun of like that, it's three brothers who were named after pickup trucks."

Elizabeth nodded back. "I can imagine."

"Those girls are gone now. Don't let them ruin your day," Chevy said. "I'll bet they were on the phone before they were even out of the driveway telling anyone who'd listen that you and my brother really are together. Heck, anyone who sees you two together can tell how durn-fool crazy you are about each other."

A shy smile crept across her face. She wished that were true. She was sure it was obvious from her. She'd never been good at hiding her feelings, but she knew Ford was just saying all that stuff because he was a nice guy and to put her cousins in their place.

She snuck a quick glance and caught him smiling at her. She had to look away, swallowing at the emotion burning her throat, because his smile wasn't the coy, flirty kind from earlier, but a tender one that had her heart wishing this relationship was real.

It was after eight that night, and Ford and Elizabeth had just finished prepping the kitchen and the cabinet doors to paint. He'd been pleased when so many friends and neighbors had shown up to pitch in that day. And even more pleased at the massive amount of progress they'd made.

"I can't believe how much we got done today," Elizabeth said, as if mirroring his thoughts.

"We have a saying in the country…make hay while the sun shines. Several of those folks said they were coming back out tomorrow to help paint. So, if you feel good about your color choices, I say we pick up paint in the morning and let 'em rip. If enough of them show up again, we might get the whole interior painted tomorrow."

"That would be amazing. I figured it would take weeks for me to paint this place by myself."

"Good thing you're not by yourself," he reminded her, then couldn't help but smile at the soft pink that colored her cheeks. He liked the way she blushed, especially if that pink was caused by a compliment he'd given her or by something flirty he'd said.

"I love the look of crisp white for all the trim, and I'm really happy with that light gray color I picked for the walls. The old me would probably spend another two months debating the different shades of gray, going back and forth between gray blue and gray-beige, and then second-guessing my choices. But the new me is all about making choices and sticking with them. I was in a client's house earlier this year who used the same color gray throughout their interior, and it was gorgeous, so I'm just going with it."

"It's a great color. I'm sure it will look nice." He held up the sprayer. "Speaking of paint. What do you think? Are you ready to call it a night? Or do you want to stick it out and get the kitchen and these cabinets painted?"

She looked over at the taped kitchen, then down at the row of cabinet faces lined up in the living room. "If you're up for it, I say we push on."

"I'm good. I think if you work on painting the cabinet frames, I can spray the doors, then we can knock out the little bit of wall space together. Everything will be dry when we come back in the morning, and you already picked out the hardware, so we can put the doors and the handles on, and I'll bet your cabinets will be done by noon."

A big smile spread across her face, and she clapped her hands together. "I'm so excited. But we're well past a normal workday, and I don't want to take advantage of you. Are you sure you're up for a few more hours?"

He had put together a quote for her that morning, outlining the main renovations, including paint, lumber, plumbing, demo, labor, supplies, and his fee as the contractor. She'd argued with him at first since his fee was so much lower than Chad Douche-Nugget's had been. She wanted to pay him a fair rate, but he was trying to save her money.

They talked through her budget for the renovation, and then had eventually settled on an amount for his contractor fee that would just cover the cost of the new farm implement they needed at the ranch, which seemed to make them both happy.

"I'm good," he told her. "You're paying me for the

job, not by the hour, and I'd like to get this finished up tonight too."

In truth, he was hoping to completely wear himself out. When he fell into bed that night, he wanted to be so tired that he'd fall right to sleep, instead of spending hours awake, like he'd done the night before, thinking about the lush body in the bed next to him.

He was still a little shocked at how quickly things had escalated earlier that day. It had started with just one kiss. She'd been driving him crazy all morning, and he'd kept finding ways to touch her, to brush against her soft skin, to sneak glances at her. She had on a pair of faded jean shorts and a simple white tank top that hugged her perfect breasts, and even though tendrils of curls kept escaping her loosely knotted pony tail, she still looked gorgeous to him.

He hadn't meant to kiss her, but when she'd practically fallen into his arms, it felt so amazing to have her there. He'd just wanted one taste of her—just one sample of her sweet lips—but she'd tasted too good and the scent of her swirled around him, and one kiss wasn't enough. Not when she was clutching his back and arching into him. Not when he was finally able to touch her, to fill his hands with her sumptuous curves. Hell, he'd been ready to strip her naked and take her on the kitchen counter.

He wasn't sure what would have happened if his brother hadn't walked in. And he wasn't sure if he could keep his hands off her if she curled up to him again tonight. She was too tempting, too luscious, too enticing. He knew he needed to back off, to not let his feelings for her overcome him, but his control was slipping.

Focus on the house. Concentrate on the task at hand.

"Let's do this," he said, reaching for a can of paint. "Your dream kitchen is almost here."

She clapped her hands together again. "Yes. We've still got a little sun left, so let's make hay."

Three hours later, they finally made it back to the ranch. Elizabeth's shoulders were aching and there was a smear of paint across her arm and probably some in her hair, but she didn't care.

The walls of the kitchen were now a soft gray. The top cabinets were a creamy white and the bottom ones were a gorgeous shade of navy blue. She could already imagine how the white and gray marbled quartz countertops she'd chosen would look and the new stainless-steel appliances would bring the whole beautiful kitchen together.

She was so tired, she'd thought she wouldn't be able to keep her eyes open, but the sound of the water running in the bathroom and the image of Ford in the shower, water racing down his hard muscled body, was keeping her wide awake.

She closed her eyes, willing herself to sleep, but all she could focus on was the sound of the water stopping and imagining him toweling off and being jealous of the fabric that got to run over the muscles of his arms and chest.

The door to the bathroom opened a few minutes later, releasing a cloud of steam into the room scented with soap, toothpaste, and whatever amazing-smelling body wash he used. She opened her eyes in time to catch sight of him, naked except for a pair of boxer briefs, before he snapped off the bedside light and climbed into bed with her.

The mattress dipped, and every nerve in her body tingled at the nearness of him. She ached to reach out, to run her fingers over his firm biceps, to brush her hands over the bare skin of his chest, to have him pull her close and kiss her with the abandon he'd had earlier in the day on the kitchen counter.

She loved the colors and the textures she was using to create her dream kitchen, but one of her favorite parts about it would always be the memories of Ford stripping her shirt off and pressing her against the counter, gripping her hips and feeling his need for her as he pulled her against him.

He adjusted his body in the bed, punching his pillow into a different shape and letting out a huff as he shifted into a new position.

Even though she wasn't touching him, she could still feel the tenseness of his frame. Was he nervous? Annoyed?

She wanted to talk to him, needed to talk about the weekend they'd spent together and how they'd left so many things unsaid. This probably wasn't the best time. They were both tired. But it didn't seem like Ford was drifting off to sleep either.

One part of her screamed to put this discussion off, to just enjoy the feeling of being Ford's girlfriend. Even if it wasn't real.

The way he touched her and occasionally kissed her when they were in front of other people felt so good. Those moments seemed worth ignoring this discussion and the chance that she might wreck everything and lose even his fake attention.

But what if they talked about the weekend, and she admitted her feelings were real? She already knew that Ford wasn't into relationships, so by telling him how she felt, she could risk losing even the pretend relationship they had. She didn't even know if a relationship was what she was really looking for. She'd made so many big changes already.

But she knew she wanted *something* with him. Something that involved being able to kiss him and touch him and do things in his bed other than just sleep.

Which is what she should be doing now. She should let them *both* get a good night's rest. She could rethink her strategy in the morning then talk to him tomorrow. Or the next day. Or never.

These were all the things her mind was saying, but her body overrode those things as her hand reached out and touched Ford's shoulder.

"Hey," she whispered. "Can we talk?"

CHAPTER FOURTEEN

ELIZABETH HELD HER breath. Now she'd done it.

"Sure," Ford said, still facing away from her. "What do you want to talk about? Because I was just thinking about how we could make an arched opening in your bedroom and not have to tear down the whole wall. That way we could keep the strength of the walls if they are structural. And when we rip out the opening, we might find some of that shiplap you wanted, and we could expose that for the arched wall."

That was what he was thinking about? At least his mind was *somewhere* in the vicinity of her bedroom. Just not in the same way hers was.

"No. I mean, yes, that all sounds amazing," she said. "But I wanted to talk about something else. Something that's been bothering me."

"Oh-kay." He drew the word out as he rolled over to face her. The room was dark, but there was enough moonlight coming through the window to still see his face and read his expressions. "What's on your mind?"

"I owe you an apology."

"An apology? What for?"

"For standing you up for breakfast that last day of the wedding weekend. For driving away without saying goodbye. For being too chicken to face you and talk about what happened."

His eyes widened then he shook his head. "That stuff doesn't matter anymore."

"It matters to me."

"Why?"

"Because it was wrong. Because I shouldn't have left you without talking to you or at least saying goodbye."

"Wouldn't be the first time that's happened to me."

"I know. That's why I need to apologize. I'm not like that. And I don't want to be just one more person in your life who left."

He shrugged one shoulder. "If you wouldn't have, I would have eventually."

"Ouch."

"Sorry. I'm not trying to sound like a jerk. I'm just no good at relationships."

"Unless they're fake?" She offered him a coy smile. "Because this pretend one has been pretty amazing. Especially earlier today. In the kitchen."

"You know that wasn't fake." He reached up and brushed a lock of hair from her forehead, the feel of his fingers grazing her skin sending shivers down her arms. "I do like you, Elizabeth. I like you a lot. And I liked what we were doing in the kitchen today. And I *loved* what we did the weekend we spent together. I told your cousins that I have a hard time keeping my hands off you, and that's true." He closed his eyes for a moment and made a growling sound in his throat. "In fact, I'm having a hell of a time right now, because all I want to do is strip you naked and kiss every inch of your body."

She drew in a quick breath. "Okay," she whispered.

He let out a soft sound that was part laugh, part anguish. "You're killin' me darlin'."

Her brows drew together. "Why? You keep saying these things that make me think you want me, but then you back off. I don't understand."

"Damn it. I *do* want you. I want you with every breath I take. I want you every time our hands touch or I smell the scent of you. But it's because I *do* like you that I'm *not* tearing your clothes off. I'm just… *not* the kind of man you want. I'm not the guy that sticks around. And I don't want to hurt you."

"Does it matter what *I* want?"

"Yeah, of course. Tell me. What do you want? And I'm not talking about what you want right now, in this bed…" He lowered his gaze to her chest and just the heat and hunger in his eyes made her nipples tighten. "Although, I'm game to talk about that later, but you've got a lot going on right now, so what do *you* want?"

She sighed. It was hard to think clearly—and about anything *other* than his comment about tearing her clothes off—but she understood what he was asking. And talking this through was what she'd intended when she started this whole conversation.

"I don't know. I know that I've made all these big changes in my life, taken steps that I never thought I'd have the courage to take. I'm trying to reach out and grab the things I've always wanted. Things I've been too afraid to reach for, or that I didn't think I deserved. I've made this huge commitment by taking on this house, and there are a million things to do. Not just the renovations, but moving my stuff up here, unpacking, picking out rugs and pictures, and setting up the freaking wi-fi. I'm going to be working remotely for the first time ever, so I need to create a functional home office, but I've also got a yard full of weeds and *a barn*. What am I supposed to do with a barn? I just feel like all my focus needs to be on the house and figuring out my new life."

"Then that's what you need to focus on."

"But all I can think about is you. And all that tearing our clothes off stuff."

He grinned. "I think about you too." He let out a long sigh. "So help me, I think about you all the time. Thoughts of that weekend have kept me up at night for the past month. And now that you're here again, all I want to do is kiss you, and touch you, and fill my hands with your gorgeous ass."

She swallowed. No one had ever spoken to her with the kinds of words Ford used…stripping her naked, thinking about the scent of her, filling his hands with her. His words created an ache in her like she'd never felt before. And a white-hot desire to let him do everything he'd said. *And more.*

She lowered her chin and then looked up at him through her lashes. Her voice was breathy as she told him, "I want those things too." She reached for the hem of his T-shirt, but he put his hand over hers and held it in place.

"We can't. *I* can't."

"I don't understand. You just said that you think

about me…" A hard realization dawned on her, and a knot of shame twisted in her chest. "Oh. I get it. You just don't think about me like *that*. Because I'm, you know…" She couldn't bring herself to say fuller-figured or curvy or any of the other words she used to describe her thicker thighs and wider hips. "I know you're probably used to being with women who are more like my cousin, the *real* Elizabeth."

He frowned. "First of all, you *are* the real Elizabeth. You're the one I always wanted to be with. The only reason I agreed when Brody asked me to hang out with his cousin for the weekend was because I'd already met you and liked you. It was *his* mistake that he was thinking of Liz. Not mine."

"Oh."

"And also, I do think of you like *that*. *Exactly* like that. I think you're beautiful…" He put his hand on her waist and slid it over her hip. "And your amazing body is what has me thinking about *that* with *you* every day and every night." He frowned and pulled his hand back to scrub it across his head. "But there is *no* kind of woman I'm used to being with, because I'm not used to being with women long enough to know what kind of woman they are. That's what I'm trying to tell you. I'm not the guy who stays. I'm the guy that women have fun with, then when things start to get too serious, I cut and run."

"You mean you leave before someone else can leave you?"

Ford shrugged. "I guess." He looked away. "Whatever. My point is that I think you're remarkable. You're sweet and kind and smart and funny. And so damn beautiful. I've never known anyone like you. That's why I can't let this really happen between us. Because no one's ever made me feel like you do, and I don't want to hurt you."

"Then don't."

"But I will. I know what I do." He rolled away from her and sat up on the side of the bed.

"Wait," she said, sitting up next to him and reaching for his hand. She pulled him back around, so he was facing her then pointed to the pendant at her neck. "Do you remember when you gave this to me?"

A sheepish grin played across his lips. "Yeah. I do. And I couldn't believe it when I saw you wearing it yesterday."

"You told me that this shooting star was to remind me of the night we watched the meteor shower. Which, by the way, ranks as one of the top ten best nights of my life. But you also said it was to remind me to go for the things that I want and to just do one brave thing at a time." She pressed her hand to his cheek. "Well, *you* are what I want. And this is me doing one brave thing. I don't care about what happened with the other women in your life. I care about us. And tonight. And I guess tomorrow. But I'm not asking you for anything more than that. Just one day at a time."

"But—"

She pressed her fingers to his mouth. "No buts. I'm not asking you for any promises. I'm not asking you for a relationship. I'm making changes in my life and taking risks. And this is a risk I'm willing to take. I'm not standing on the sidelines of my life anymore. I'm going for what I want. If it works out, great. If not, at least I tried."

His brows knit together as if he were in pain as he reached up and touched her cheek. "What if I hurt you?"

She shrugged and drew closer to him. Her voice was a whisper. "What if you do?"

"I couldn't take it."

"I can't take not having your hands on me, your mouth on mine. The ache I feel for you right now hurts way more than the pain you *may* cause me later."

He let out another of his anguish-filled sighs as he stared at her, looking into her eyes as if trying to see into the very depths of her.

She held her breath as she waited for him to answer.

He didn't say anything.

Instead, he wrapped his arm around her waist and pulled her to him, then crushed his mouth against hers. Instead of words, he conveyed his answer by satisfying his earlier desire of filling his hands with her and kissing every part of her. He stripped off her pajama top then laid her back against the pillows, keeping himself upright so he could feast his eyes on her.

His greedy gaze traveled over her, then he dipped his head and kissed her neck, starting at the spot just below her ear then moving down her chest. He cupped her breast, grazing the tightened nub of her nipple with his thumb before circling it with his tongue.

Heat coiled inside her as his head moved lower, trailing warm kisses over her belly, along the waistline of her pajama shorts. Then he hooked his thumbs under the elastic band and stripped away both her shorts and underwear, leaving her naked and exposed, as he gently spread her legs and kissed the inside of her thigh.

She let out a sound, something between a gasp and a moan, a sound that meant 'I can't believe how amazing that feels,' and 'please don't ever stop'.

CHAPTER FIFTEEN

ELIZABETH FELL INTO the pleasure of Ford's touch as he teased and tortured her in the most delicious ways, drawing her close to release then backing off. He ravaged her body—tasting, licking, sucking, caressing—both tender and rough as he took her cues and gave her more than she could have ever asked for. He reveled in every curve and dip of her body, making her feel like a goddess.

He wasn't the only one who got to touch and devour. Finally able to get her hands, and her mouth, on him, she explored his hard, muscled body, touching and stroking, and loving every growling groan he made because of something she did to him. He made her feel sexy and seductive, beautiful and wanton, and she loved every second of it.

Ford pulled away, just long enough to reach into the drawer of his bedside table and retrieve a foil packet. Even though she loved watching him, drinking in his sculptured body as he ripped the packet open and covered himself, her skin ached for the contact of his.

Her breath caught as he eased himself back down onto the bed and between her legs. She'd never felt this way about another man, never let herself go with such reckless abandon as she had the weekend she'd spent with him, as she was doing now. She let out a desperate moan, clinging to him as she arched and lifted her body to take him.

Heat raced through her veins as they moved together, finding their rhythm, at first soft and slow, then building to a hungry desire. She lost all sense of time, all sense of reason. The only thing that mattered was this man and the mindless delirium of his touch.

His muscles were taut as if trying to exercise restraint while the friction intensified and aching need surged inside her. Finally, in a wash of bliss and release, she cried out as she shattered around him. At the same time, he pulled her tight, clutching her to him, his voice husky and raw, growling her name into her neck as he found his own release.

In a tangle of sheets, he collapsed next to her. His breath was shaky as he pulled her close, and she clung to his chest, pressing a kiss to the side of his neck.

They could tell themselves they were pretending in front of other people, but this was real. This was more than a casual roll in the hay. It had been more that first weekend they'd been together, and it was more now.

She could talk tough, say things about not making promises, but this, being with him like this, letting him into her soul, this was a connection.

He'd warned her—flat out told her that he was going to hurt her—but she'd barreled on, because being with him, like this, felt worth the risk.

Deep down, she knew that not only could Ford Lassiter hurt her...he could splinter her into a million pieces.

But in this moment—in this place of being nestled against him, held in the circle of his arms with his lips pressing a kiss against her hair—she didn't even care.

In the morning, Elizabeth wondered if perhaps she and Ford might have been a little too loud the night before, since neither Duke nor Ford's brothers could seem to meet her eyes. Ford must have noticed too, because he suggested they grab breakfast at the diner while they were in town getting more supplies for the day.

With so much help, they wanted to make sure they had enough paint and brushes. Elizabeth had picked a softer dove gray color for her bedroom and a crisp ultra-white for all the trim and crown molding. She told Ford that she'd always wanted a super-feminine room with pink walls and white curtains, and had considered painting her home office pink, but instead went with a more professional look and stuck with the gray.

"But I am getting one can of pink paint to eventually use in the attic room. I also ordered all rose-gold office supplies for my desk," she told him as they were finishing breakfast.

They'd been working on master lists for what they needed to do in the next few days. After spending so much of the day before directing all their helpers, he'd created specific task lists for things that could be done by anyone who stopped by to help.

She'd brought her laptop and had ordered several items for the house while they were waiting for their food. Going from a tiny one-bedroom apartment to a three-bedroom house left her in need of a lot of things.

"I think I'll be getting to know the mailman and the UPS guy really well with all these boxes I'm getting delivered," she said. "I'm going to try to get some secondhand furniture, but I did order a new flannel sheet and comforter set since it's cooler in the mountains, some stuff for the kitchen, a couple of lamps for the living room, and some gorgeous floral cushions and pillows for the window seat in the attic. I have no idea when I'll get to that room, but I saw these cushions and they were so perfect, I just had to get them. Now I'll have them ready when I get a chance to work on the attic."

Ford just grinned at her. "It's good to be prepared."

He'd been grinning at her all morning. Her smile was a little shy as she grinned back. "You sure have been smiling a lot this morning."

He huffed out a laugh and rubbed at his cheek. "I know. My face isn't used it."

She laughed with him. "They say your muscles get stronger the more you use them. So, we'll just have to keep doing whatever it is that's making you smile so much."

"That's a workout I can get behind." This time his grin was flirty and accompanied by a slight arch of his eyebrow.

Heat bloomed in her chest, and she imagined her

neck and cheeks had just turned red. His innuendo had her thoughts going to that very scenario. She tried to think of something cute and clever to say back, but she was new to this whole flirt-talking thing and wasn't sure the best way to respond to his insinuation.

Thankfully, the waitress arrived with the check, saving her from saying something embarrassing.

"Everything was great. Thanks Luce," Ford told the waitress, handing her his card.

The server looked to be somewhere in her thirties, with shiny black hair pulled up into a high ponytail and black eyeliner that was drawn into perfect wings. Her name tag read "Luciana", and she smiled at Elizabeth as she took Ford's debit card and ran it through her machine. "How's the work coming out at the farmhouse?"

"Um…good," Elizabeth answered, surprised the woman knew about her house.

She shrugged as if able to read Elizabeth's mind. "I heard you had a bunch of people show up to help yesterday. Some were truly there to pitch in, but some were there just to meet the woman who finally stole Ford Lassiter's heart, and some to see what you're doing with Frank and Ida's house."

Elizabeth's chest warmed at the comment about stealing Ford's heart. Then she remembered that their relationship was all a ruse, and the only thing she'd taken from Ford Lassiter was the last bite of his syrup-soaked pancake. "Our goal is to update it, while still keeping the original feel and personality of the farmhouse," she answered, leaving out any response to the part about Ford's heart.

"My abuela was out there helping yesterday." She held her hand to her shoulder. "Short little Puerto Rican woman who swears like a sailor but can clean anything to within an inch of its life."

Elizabeth smiled. "Do you mean Miss Mariana? I'm not sure if she was cussing, but now that you mention it, she might have been swearing in Spanish at the baseboards she was scrubbing. And she brought us some tamales."

Luciana grinned. "That's her. And her tamales are legendary."

"I can't wait to try them," Elizabeth said. "It was so nice of her, and everyone, who came out to help me yesterday."

"That's a small town for you," Luciana said, tearing off a receipt and passing it and the debit card back to Ford. "People pitch in when someone needs help. I think she said she and her friends are planning to come out and help again after church this afternoon."

"They made a huge difference yesterday," Elizabeth said. "I couldn't have done all that without them. I just wish I could do something to thank them."

"You will," Luciana said, offering her an encouraging smile. "There will come a time when you're needed, and I'm sure you'll step in to help."

An hour later, after another trip to the hardware store and one to the mercantile to get her a new pair of brown and teal Roper cowboy boots, Ford pulled up in front of the farmhouse. He surveyed the work that had already been done. Chevy and his guys were almost finished with replacing the front porch, and someone must have been doing some weeding, because the yard didn't look quite as woebegone as it had the day before. There might even be some decent grass under all those weeds.

"I can't believe this is *my* house," Elizabeth said, staring through the windshield.

"Scary?"

She nodded. "Terrifying. But also exciting. The first time I drove up here, I wanted to cry. All I saw was this rundown farmhouse with peeling paint and a sagging porch, and I couldn't believe I'd sunk most of my savings into this neglected property. But it feels different now."

"I don't know. That paint is still pretty bad, but the porch *is* looking better."

She smiled. "It's not just that. Now I can see beyond the shabby. Thanks to you, and so many people who came out to help yesterday, I can see the potential of this place. I can imagine how the house will look with fresh paint and green grass and the little white picket fence back in place. I can see myself cooking in the kitchen and soaking in that awesome bathtub and sitting out back in a lawn chair appreciating the view. I didn't even know there *was* a gorgeous river that ran behind my house."

"That's because the trees and bushes are so overgrown, you can barely see it."

"Which would have made me sad before, but now I know that all it will take is a few weeks of yard work, and my backyard can be amazing."

"I think you'd be surprised at how fast some hedge

clippers and a chain saw could restore your view of the river and the mountain behind it."

Thor, who had been sitting in her lap, stood on his hind legs and put his front feet on the dashboard, as if looking at the house with them. He gave a short woof, and his tail wagged happily behind him.

"And Thor loves it," she said. "Which was one of my main objectives."

Ford nodded. "I remember…to give your dog a better life." He nodded to the farmyard. "I can't think of a better life for a dog."

"He already seems so happy here." Elizabeth let out a sigh, keeping her gaze focused on the house, so she didn't give away that any of her feelings had to do with the man sitting in the truck next to her. "So do I."

"I hope you still feel that way after ten hours of painting."

She beamed a smile in his direction. "I can't wait. And speaking of paint, the cabinet doors should all be dry by now and ready to be put back on, shouldn't they?"

"Yeah. I thought we'd do that first thing, then the kitchen will be practically finished."

"The new appliances get delivered tomorrow," she told him. "And the countertop guys said they'd try to come out to measure today."

"That farmhouse sink you ordered should be here by the time they're ready, and they'll put it in when they install the countertops. It helped that you already had the quartz in mind that you wanted."

They each grabbed a can of paint from the back of the truck and headed around to the back of the house. Elizabeth was thinking about how great it would be to have the porch finished and be able to use the front door again, and almost ran into Ford when he stopped in front of her.

"What the hell?" He put his hand out. "Stay back."

"What's wrong?" She leaned around him, and fear shot through her.

She gasped at the sight of the open back door and the cracked and broken screen door hanging from only the top hinge.

CHAPTER SIXTEEN

ELIZABETH COULDN'T QUITE grasp what she was seeing. It looked like someone had kicked the door in.

"Oh my gosh. Did someone break in?" She thought of all Ford's tools they'd left inside, and prayed they hadn't been stolen. "Do you think Chad did this?"

"I wouldn't put it past the guy. But I hope not."

"I haven't really moved anything in, so if they stole anything, it would belong to you." She gripped his arm as another thought struck her. "What if it was vandals? What if they wrecked all the hard work we did yesterday? Or worse." She imagined the freshly washed walls covered in spray painted graffiti.

Ford frowned as he shook his head. "We don't have a lot of vandalism in Woodland Hills. Maybe it was just kids who didn't realize the place wasn't empty anymore."

He took a step toward the house then stopped again as a crash sounded from inside. Ford set the paint can in the grass and cautiously approached the door. "Stay here," he whispered.

"No way," she whispered back, sticking right on his heels.

The inner door stood ajar, but she couldn't see anything inside as Ford carefully pulled open the hanging screen door. He slipped inside the mud room. She followed close behind him, one hand holding onto the back of his shirt.

Ford's boots were quiet as he eased into the kitchen, and Elizabeth peered around his shoulder. There were no immediate signs of destruction, none of the spray paint Elizabeth feared would be on the walls, and all of Ford's tools seemed to still be in their rightful place on the designated tool table.

The settee had been turned to face the view out the window, and what Elizabeth did see was a trail of trash from the snacks and food they'd left on the counter leading toward the small sofa. A crumpled bag from some Cheetos, the empty plastic bag that had once held hamburger buns, a mangled package of Oreos.

A sound like a snort came from that same direction, and the settee shifted just the slightest.

Ford moved slowly toward the sofa, making a wide circle around the room. Elizabeth realized she was still holding a paint can and tightened her grip on the handle, ready to swing the heavy can at the intruder.

When they had first gotten out of the truck, Thor and Dixie had sped off to sniff and explore the yard and take care of their business. With a bang, they both now came through the hole of the dangling screen door and raced into the kitchen.

Dixie stopped, lowered her body, and let out a snarling growl. But Thor, the small dog with the heart of a warrior, went tearing across the room, barking his head off as he circled the settee.

A frightened whinny rang through the air as Elizabeth and Ford rounded the sofa to see a tiny donkey scrambling back into the corner of the settee.

"Thor! Get back." Elizabeth reached for the dog's collar as she tried to comprehend the fact that a baby donkey had broken into her house and apparently eaten a snack of Cheetos, Oreos, and hamburger buns. The dog ignored her and jumped onto the other end of the sofa, which caused the donkey to whinny again as it scrambled down and headed straight for Elizabeth.

She dropped the can of paint and ran toward Ford, trying to dodge the animal. But the donkey raced after her. She shrieked and ran around the sofa. The donkey was hot on her heels, and Dixie and Thor must have thought this was a fun game, because they joined in the chase, barking as they ran.

As if she were trying to get away from a mouse, she jumped up on the sofa. "Help me," she called to Ford.

He made a grab for the little donkey, but it escaped his grasp and ran another circle around the settee. "What do you want me to do?" he yelled over the cacophony of barking, whinnying, and loud clops of hooves on the hardwood floor.

"Grab some more snacks and try to lure it outside," she yelled back. She wasn't sure, but for a second there, she thought he might be laughing. "Are you laughing? Do you think is funny?" She shrieked again as the donkey tried to scramble onto the sofa with her.

She wasn't sure if it was trying to get *to* her or just get *away* from the dogs. They weren't trying to hurt the donkey, as much as play with it.

It butted its big ears into her legs, and she leapt from the sofa.

It jumped down too.

"Find some more cookies," she yelled to Ford. She stuck out her hands to ward off the donkey whose eyes were wide and scared as it headed right toward her.

Her feet got tangled as she ran into the paint can she'd dropped, and she stumbled backward and fell on her butt. Covering her face with her hands, she waited for the attack from the donkey.

Instead of the harsh scrape of hooves and gnashing teeth she expected, the small donkey rubbed the furry knot on its head against Elizabeth's arm and tried to nuzzle into the crook of her shoulder.

"Aww." She looked up at Ford as she reached out and gently petted the baby animal. Its coat was a spotted brown and white, and Elizabeth couldn't believe how soft it was. The donkey was trembling as it pushed closer against her. "It's shaking."

"I'll bet she is," Ford said.

"She?"

Ford nodded. "Yes. And she's probably terrified. Can you imagine? She was just sitting here on the sofa, minding her own business, having a snack of some Oreos and bread, when all these people and dogs come in here and start barking and hollering. Wouldn't you be terrified?"

Elizabeth stroked the little donkey's head. "You're right," she told Ford. "The poor thing. I probably didn't help the situation either. I was just surprised. And I'll admit to being a little scared. I'm not used to finding farmyard animals in my living room."

"None of us are," he said.

"Where did she come from? Is she a baby? And if so, do we need to be worried about the mama-donkey charging in here to find her?"

"She's not a baby. She's just a miniature donkey."

"Oh my gosh. How adorable. You mean this is a big as she gets?"

"That would be my guess, yes," he said, giving the donkey's ears a scratch before pulling back her lips and looking at her teeth. "Oh yeah, she's at least ten years old."

Elizabeth peered into the donkey's mouth. "How do you know?"

"You can tell the approximate age of a horse, or in this case, a donkey, by the eruption and wear patterns of their teeth."

"I'm impressed."

He shrugged. "I've been a rancher for most of my life. Horses and cattle are my livelihood. And my grandpa was a good teacher."

The donkey had now curled on her side, pressed up against Elizabeth's leg and rested her head on her thigh. She and Dixie and Thor had all sniffed and inspected each other, and Thor crawled into Elizabeth's lap and put his head down next to the donkey's. Dixie plopped down on the floor next to the animal, and Elizabeth noted the mini donkey was about the same size as the golden retriever.

Elizabeth took turns trying to pet all three animals. "Do you have any idea where she came from?"

Ford shook his head. "No clue. I don't recognize her."

"What is she doing here?"

"You mean besides eating all our snack food?"

Elizabeth laughed. "Yes."

"Again. No clue."

"Well, do you have a clue about what we should do with her? Or how we can find out where she belongs?"

"I guess I could check the Donkey Directory."

Her eyes widened. "They have one of those?"

He laughed and shook his head. "No. They do *not* have one of those. I was just teasing. But Duke is planning to bring over lunch again, and we're expecting a bunch of people to show up to help with the house. Maybe one of them might know who she belongs to."

"Good idea." She peered down at the mini donkey, who had scooched closer and was now practically in her lap. "I guess I'll just have to sit here and cuddle this adorable little creature until then."

"What about putting the cupboard doors back on in the kitchen?"

She sighed. "Who needs cabinet doors when they have a mini donkey in their lap?"

Ford chuckled. "I see your point. I'll go out and grab the rest of the paint and supplies while you resume snuggling up with the farmyard animal."

"Sounds great."

But when Ford headed for the door, the dogs got up to follow, and then so did the little donkey. They formed a tiny pet parade as they trailed after him into the yard. Elizabeth laughed as she pushed up off the floor and took her place at the end of the line.

The animals followed them in and out of the house as they brought in the supplies, pausing occasionally to romp in the grass or take care of their animal business.

"Is it possible that donkey is house-trained?" Elizabeth asked as she held a cabinet door up so Ford could screw the hinge back in place.

"Oh yeah. Donkeys are really smart. And those little miniature ones are known to be great pets. They're good with kids, super social, and like you can tell with this one, they love affection. And their average life span is like thirty years, so they live a long time compared to most pets."

"Thirty *years*? I got a hamster once, and he didn't even make it thirty *days*."

Ford and Elizabeth stood back to admire their work. The new cupboard doors were all in place, and they looked amazing.

"I can't believe how different the kitchen already looks," Elizabeth told him as she ran her hand over the crisp white surface. "You were so right about painting the cabinets. This saved me so much money. Thank you."

"The color choices were yours, so you should take the credit for how great the space looks now."

"How about we share the credit?" she said, turning and wrapping her arms around his waist. "How should we celebrate the completion of the cabinets?"

He grinned. "I don't usually celebrate the

completion of a home improvement project, but I'm open to suggestions. What do you have in mind?" He hugged her to him then his hands slipped over her hips to cup her generous butt.

Leaning in, she pressed a kiss to his neck. It was just a soft graze of her lips, but his body instantly responded. Heat surged through his veins, and he hauled her against him and captured her mouth in a kiss that he hoped conveyed how much he wanted her. And if his kiss didn't, other parts of his body were certainly communicating the message.

She ground her hips against those *other* parts, and a growl hummed in his throat as he lifted her up onto the kitchen countertop. She wrapped her legs around his waist as she deepened his next kiss. He palmed her back with one hand while the other slid under her shirt and over the smooth bare skin of her stomach to tease the lacy edge of her bra.

CHAPTER SEVENTEEN

THE BLOOD IN Ford's veins ran hot. The feel of Elizabeth's body in his hands had been all he could think about that morning. Well, until they discovered the tiny farmyard intruder. Then his body had gone into protector mode.

But after, when they were installing the cabinet doors, watching her move, the fluid ease of her limbs, the tiny peeks of skin he got when she raised her arms, the flash of her smile—she'd been driving him crazy.

The night before, in his bed, had been amazing. Better than all the times he'd been imagining having her there. This morning, he hadn't wanted to push or act like he expected anything. He was trying to let her take the lead. He was proud of her for standing up for what she wanted, for stepping out of her comfort zone, and damn happy to oblige if one of those brave steps she'd been talking about taking happened to be getting naked with him.

Her skin was so soft. She smelled so amazing. Before he could really start showing her how *excited* he was about finishing those kitchen cabinets, he heard car doors slam and the sound of voices out front.

Seriously?

He groaned as he pulled his hand out of Elizabeth's shirt and took a step back, adjusting himself so whoever had just shown up wouldn't be able to see the evidence of their 'celebrating'.

She laughed as she hopped off the counter. "Apparently, we are not meant to christen these countertops. Maybe we're supposed to wait for the new ones to come in."

"Promises, promises," he muttered as he heard the back screen door creak then his grandfather's voice boom into the room.

"What in tarnation happened to your screen door?" Duke bellowed, walking into the kitchen. His arms were laden with two stacked cardboard boxes that filled the air with the scent of his famous fried chicken.

Ford hurried toward him to take the boxes. The dogs and the donkey, who had been napping together in a patch of sunlight on the floor, all leapt up and raced across the room to greet Duke. "Our new house guest happened," he said as he placed the boxes on the counter. "She was inside when we got here a few hours ago. Do you know who she belongs to?"

Duke shook his head as he took turns scratching the ears of all three animals. "I can't say that I do, but she's a cute little bugger."

"What's Vera doing here?" Ruby Foster asked as she and Maisie arrived a few minutes later.

The little donkey brayed and raced toward the older woman.

"Vera?" Elizabeth asked. "Ruby, do you know who this donkey belongs to?"

"Sure, I do," Ruby said, giving the donkey's ears a scratch. "She's Bette Thompson's. Bette got her after her husband died about ten years ago. She talked about getting a dog, but decided she wanted a companion that would outlive her. So, she got Vera, and that little donkey has been the best thing to happen to her. She loves Bette. She's so affectionate and follows Bette everywhere. She's even house-trained and sleeps in a crate at night like a dog would."

"Oh, I'm so glad to know who she belongs to. We found her in the house this morning." Elizabeth decided not to mention the snack food raid. Her owner might not be too thrilled that Vera had ingested half a bag of Oreos and a significant amount of Crunchy Cheetos. "If you tell us where she lives, we can take her home."

"She lives across the road and up a ways," Ruby said. "But you can't take her home. Bette's not there. She fell last week and broke her hip. She's in a rehabilitation center right now."

"Oh no. Do you think Vera was left in the house alone? No wonder she broke in here. She was probably starving. And worried about Bette."

Ruby shook her head. "Even if she was dying, Bette wouldn't neglect Vera. I'm sure she asked someone to check in on her. Maybe she ran away."

"Do you have a way to contact Bette? She's probably worried sick. And that can't be good for her recovery."

"No, I imagine not." Ruby pulled her phone from her handbag. "I can try her number. If she doesn't answer, we can try the rehab center."

Thankfully, Bette did answer, and Elizabeth listened as Ruby explained the situation to her.

"She wants to talk to you," Ruby said, holding the phone out to Elizabeth.

"Me?" She took the phone and hesitantly held it up to her ear. "Hello?"

"Oh hi, honey. This is Bette Thompson. I'm so grateful you found my Vera. I've been in this dang rehab place for three days now, and I've been worried sick about her. I asked a neighbor to go check on her, and to put her in the barn, but she gets so lonely by herself. She always prefers the house."

"Do you want us to take her back there? Or put her in your barn?"

"Oh no. Please don't. She must have been so sad on her own that she escaped the barn and found her way to your house. And Ruby said she likes you."

"How can she tell?"

"Oh, she can tell. Vera's a persnickety little thing. If she cuddles up to you, that means she likes you."

"She *is* very affectionate." The little donkey was leaning into her legs and nudging her forehead against Elizabeth's hand like she was trying to get her to pet her. Or she might have heard Bette's voice coming from the phone. "I just thought she was like that with everyone."

"Oh no. And especially not men. She's very picky about the men she lets near her. She only lets the truly kindhearted ones near her."

Elizabeth thought of the way the donkey had practically climbed into Ford's lap when he'd gotten down on the floor to play with her and the dogs. She'd nuzzled into his neck and licked his face.

"I'm so sorry that you've been hurt, Miss Bette, but I'm in the middle of a big home renovation—"

"Yes, I know," Bette said, cutting her argument off. "You bought Frank and Ida's place. Vera's been over there to visit several times before. That must be why she went to your house—because she feels safe there, which is why it would help me so much if you kept her."

Her resolve was weakening. This woman was playing into all her sympathies. But even though she'd just purchased a rundown farmhouse on a whim, Elizabeth was still the same pragmatic sensible accountant who knew she had no business taking on a pet donkey, no matter how ridiculously adorable she was. "But I don't know anything about taking care of a donkey."

"You don't have to. She really acts more like a dog," Bette assured her. "You can take care of a dog, right?"

"Well, yes—"

Bette cut her off again. "Then you can take care of Vera. I promise she won't be any bother. I'll sleep so much better here knowing that she's taken care of. I'm sure it will help my recovery too."

Come on. That last bit was a low blow. How could

even the most practical person withstand the claim that taking care of the cute donkey would help Bette recover faster?

"Maybe. I guess I could keep her for a few days."

"Thank you, honey. You'll have to run out to my house to get her food. I've got grain and hay in the barn and her treats are in the kitchen. I'll text you over the instructions for feeding her. She can just sleep on a blanket on the floor in your room, or you're welcome to take her crate with you. It's in the living room. She's such a sweetheart. I know you two will have a lot of fun together."

They would probably have more fun together if she weren't in the middle of a move and a major overhaul of a farmhouse. But she couldn't find it in her to tell the older woman 'no.'

"Don't worry about a thing. We'll take good care of her." She'd already agreed, might as well go all in. "You just focus on getting better, Miss Bette."

"Thank you so much. You're a dear. And one more thing, be careful about keeping food out on the counter. My Vera loves snacks, and cookies are her favorites."

This she did know. Especially Oreos.

Elizabeth hung up and shrugged at Ford's questioning look. "I guess we're keeping the donkey. At least until Miss Bette gets out of assisted care."

He shook his head, but she caught the grin pulling at the corner of his lips.

"It's good of you to help out," Maisie told her, bending down to give Vera's ears a scratch.

"I'm happy to share the load if you want to have her for a sleepover."

"I think I'm good for now. But I'll let you know if I change my mind."

"I'm just glad Ruby knew who she belonged to."

Maisie smiled at the older woman. "Of course, she did. My grandma knows everything about everyone."

"Ruby is your grandmother?" Elizabeth asked.

Maisie nodded. "She's my dad's mom. We rode out together today, and we brought sloppy Joes for supper. I already plugged the slow cooker in and put the hamburger buns on the counter."

Elizabeth couldn't believe the amount of food folks had brought. The refrigerator was stocked from the day before, and the counter was already filling with bags of chips, veggie trays, watermelon, and packages of cookies from the friends and neighbors arriving today.

"That's so nice of you all," she told Maisie. "But keep those hamburger buns away from Vera. Those seem to be her favorites."

With the mini donkey mystery solved, Ford and Elizabeth could focus on the next issue at hand, trying to manage all the people coming into the house. It seemed like everyone who had come out to help the day before had all returned and brought another friend or two.

Duke insisted on feeding everyone, and he and Elizabeth worked in the kitchen together, setting out lunch and snacks and washing dishes. She was thankful she and Ford had stopped at the grocery store and stocked up on paper goods and bottled water.

"I don't know how to thank you enough or repay

you for all you've done to help me," she told Duke as they were cleaning up the lunch dishes.

"You've *already* thanked me enough, and there's nothing to repay," he said. "Just seeing how happy you make my grandson is payment enough. I've never seen him smile as much as he has in the last few days. Having a girlfriend like you looks good on him."

She had to turn away. She couldn't look Duke in the eye knowing that she wasn't really Ford's girlfriend. This was all pretend. And could end any day. Ford might be smiling a lot, but that could just be because of what was happening with them in the bedroom.

They'd agreed to take things one day at a time, and today, *and last night*, had been amazing. But Ford had told her he couldn't make her any promises, and she'd never been the type of woman who could make a man do anything he didn't want to. Maybe her cousin, Liz, the *other* Elizabeth, could—with her long legs and model looks. But Elizabeth knew she was lucky to have the attention of a guy like Ford and that she should just appreciate it while it lasted. Because it could be over at any time.

After lunch was finished, Ford divided up the helpers, getting one team set up to paint the upstairs rooms and one to paint the downstairs. Chevy and his friends got back to work on the front porch, and the gardeners in the group set themselves up in the yard. They brought with them buckets and trowels and industrial lawn bags and set to weeding the yard and flower gardens, pruning the trees and bushes, and tearing out overgrown foliage.

Elizabeth made sure that Maisie and Dodge were assigned to paint one of the rooms upstairs together. She'd never considered herself any kind of matchmaker, but she thought these two needed a little push.

A friend of Ford's, who also happened to be a structural engineer, showed up and confirmed the wall in the master bedroom was not load bearing and gave them the go-ahead to knock out a section. She and Ford had talked about turning the smaller space into a closet area, and she couldn't wait to see how it turned out.

Two men from the countertop place showed up to take measurements, and the desk she'd ordered for her office was delivered. Someone must've brought a Bluetooth speaker because the house was filled with oldies music and laughter.

Elizabeth loved it all. She couldn't believe this was her life. Or her house.

Later that night, after the sloppy Joes had been eaten and the friends and neighbors had driven away, Ford and Elizabeth walked through the house.

"Wow," she said, marveling at the soft gray walls and dazzling white trim. "I can't believe how much progress we made today." The entire interior was painted, and the yard looked completely different.

"Yeah, it's amazing what you can accomplish with a group of willing hands." Ford rubbed the head of the mini donkey, who was accompanying them on their tour of the house. "We crossed so many things off our list today. Which is good, because now that the weekend's over, I don't think we'll have anyone show up tomorrow."

The front porch was completed, so they locked up and led their menagerie toward Ford's truck. Elizabeth hadn't driven her own car in days, and it was starting to just feel natural to head for the truck. They had unpacked her car the day before. Not that she had brought much beyond some of her clothes, electronic equipment, and all of Thor's things. Oh, and of course the basket of snacks that Vera had demolished that morning.

The cab of the pickup had seemed cozy with Ford, Elizabeth, and their two dogs, but adding a mini donkey caused them to squish a bit. Thor climbed onto Elizabeth's lap, and Dixie and Vera both tried to sit in the seat. That is, after Vera sniffed around the cab and used her long tongue to lick out a few crumbs from the cupholders.

An old guy they passed on the highway simply nodded as if a donkey in the front seat of a pickup was normal, but another car full of kids, hollered and waved when they caught sight of Vera through the window.

The Thompson farm was only a mile or two down the road and around the corner from Elizabeth's place. But the trek through the pastures would have been shorter for Vera.

"I've driven by here, of course, but I don't think I've been here in years," Ford said, as they pulled into the small farmyard. A faded yellow one-story farmhouse in need of a paint job sat across from a small white barn. An empty chicken coop that was all but falling down sat to the side of the house with a flourishing vegetable garden next to it.

Vera's ears perked up, and she let out a bray as

they parked then tried to scramble out of the truck. Once free, she went galloping up the porch steps and pawed at the front door.

"Oh no," Elizabeth said, pressing her hand to her mouth. "She must think Bette's inside."

The front door was unlocked, and they let themselves in to a tidy living room with a floral sofa and several bookshelves laden with books. The house smelled of vanilla and lavender, and a knitting bag overflowing with skeins of yarn sat on the floor next to the sofa. An empty cup and two saucers sat on the end table. Even though Elizabeth had never met Bette in person, she could still imagine an older woman sharing a cup of tea and two plates of dessert with the mini donkey while they watched an episode of *Downton Abbey* together.

A crate was in one corner of the room with a pink and white striped blanket and a fluffy pink stuffed unicorn inside. Vera ran around the room, sniffing at the furniture, then raced down the hallway to where Elizabeth presumed the bedrooms were. She came back and looked up at Elizabeth. Vera's tail, which had been wagging when they came in, now hung still.

"I'm sorry," Elizabeth told her, squatting down to pet the donkey. "She's not here. But hopefully you'll see her soon."

"I went to high school with a girl who works in that rehabilitation center where Miss Bette is," Ford told her. "And I'll bet I could sweet talk her into looking the other way if we wanted to sneak Vera in for a quick visit."

Elizabeth smiled up at him, and she was fairly

certain Vera did too. "I love that idea." And there was a solid chance she was falling *in* love with the guy who'd come up with it.

True to her word, Bette had texted Elizabeth with instructions for feeding the little donkey. The barley straw and grain were kept in the barn, and they found a small jar of peppermints in the kitchen, which Bette said Vera was allowed to have one each day.

The kitchen was in a bit more disarray. The sink held a stack of dirty dishes, a small saucepan sat on the stove, and the dogs and the donkey all took a turn sniffing at the trashcan that was close to overflowing.

Elizabeth nodded to the sink. "Can you wait just a few minutes so I can wash up these dishes? Then Bette can come home to a clean kitchen."

"I was thinking the same thing," Ford said. "I'll take out this trash and load the crate and the feed into the truck while you do that."

Forty minutes later, they made it back to the Lassiter Ranch. The dogs and Vera explored the ranch, and the donkey introduced herself to the horses in the barn as Ford unloaded the truck.

Duke was in the kitchen when they trooped through. He raised an eyebrow at Ford. "You haven't brought a woman to the house in years, and now not only have you got one sleeping in your bedroom, but you're also gonna have two dogs and a mini donkey in there with ya, too. Who are you and what have you done with my grandson?"

CHAPTER EIGHTEEN

THE NEXT MORNING, Elizabeth woke to the smell of coffee and bacon. She lay on her side with her back to Ford and Thor curled against her stomach. She let out a sleepy sigh, not ready to open her eyes and face the day as she rolled over to cuddle with Ford.

His warm breath hit her in the face, and she wrinkled her nose. That was some morning breath.

He nuzzled her cheek, his lips velvety soft…wait…something was off…those weren't Ford's lips…then she got another blast of hot breath. She opened her eyes and found herself staring into the deep brown eyes and very large teeth of the miniature donkey.

"Gah!" she shrieked as the donkey's long tongue slid out and licked up the side of her cheek. "Yuck."

She backpedaled away from the donkey but shoved away too hard. Her body balanced for just a moment on the edge of the bed before she slid off and landed on the floor. Thankfully, Thor had jumped off first and now ran around her head, alternately yipping at Vera and trying to lick Elizabeth's face.

Vera stood in the middle of the bed and brayed down at her. Elizabeth wasn't sure how to interpret the bray. It could have meant, "Sorry my morning breath knocked you out of bed," or "Is this a new game and should I jump down there with you to play?"

Elizabeth yelped again as a loud knock sounded at the bedroom door.

"Everything okay in there?" Dodge called through the door.

"Yes, I'm fine," she called back. "Just not used to waking up with a donkey in my bed."

She heard Dodge's bark of laughter. "That's not the worst thing I've heard said about my brother."

"No, not Ford…" she tried to say then waved a dismissive hand at the door. "Oh, forget it."

Vera plopped down on the bed and stretched out her neck to give Elizabeth another lick. But she was prepared this time and turned her cheek. She scratched Vera's forehead then pushed up from the floor to give her a little cuddle before grabbing some fresh clothes and heading for the bathroom.

The warm water felt good on her sore muscles, and she kept her eyes closed as she washed the shampoo from her hair. She heard the door click open and couldn't help the smile that curved her lips in anticipation of Ford stepping into the shower with her.

She just needed five more seconds to finish washing out the shampoo. The shower curtain rustled, and she felt him nudge the side of her thigh.

Her smile widened as she swept the water from her eyes and opened them. "Oh my lanta!" she shouted. "Vera! Get out of this shower!"

The little donkey had her chin lifted and was lapping at the water raining down from the shower head with her tongue. She pulled back her lips, so it looked like she was smiling at Elizabeth.

"We are really going to have to have a conversation about boundaries," she told the donkey as she pulled back the shower curtain and screamed again at Ford standing in the open doorway. She grabbed the curtain and pulled it around herself.

He was smiling almost as broadly as Vera had been. "I just came in to check on you, but if I'm interrupting something…"

"Oh, for heaven's sake." She huffed. "I thought she was *you* getting in the shower with me."

"I'm not sure how to take that. Should I be insulted?"

"Just help me get the donkey out of this shower before the hot water runs out."

"Come on, girl," he told the donkey. He was still grinning as he reached for her mane and shooed her out of the bathroom. "Is the offer still open for me to join you?" he called back to Elizabeth.

"I think the moment's lost." She narrowed her eyes and pointed a dripping hand at him. "And quit laughing."

"I'm laughing *with* you," he said then ducked as she threw a shower poof at him.

No cars were in the driveway when Ford and Elizabeth pulled up to her house an hour later. Ford had told her not to expect anyone to show up today, most likely because it was Monday and so much of the interior work had already been completed.

That was okay with Elizabeth. Ford also seemed happy to have the house to themselves. Well, not exactly to themselves. There were still two dogs and a miniature donkey traipsing around the place.

They had plenty of leftovers in the refrigerator and the counter was stacked with snacks, so there was no chance of them going hungry today.

They talked through their plans for the day. Elizabeth wanted to paint the French doors leading into her office, and Ford was going to work on the wall in the master bedroom. The appliances were being delivered that afternoon, and Ford and his brothers had already pulled out the stove and the dishwasher since they weren't using them. The delivery guys would take the old appliances with them, so they were waiting until they arrived to switch the things out of the refrigerator.

Dixie followed Ford upstairs, but Thor and Vera stayed on the main level with Elizabeth and supervised her work. She taped off the windowpanes then painted the doors the same crisp white as the trim.

Ford came downstairs a few hours later as she was finishing the job. She lifted her hand to suppress a yawn then swore as the bristles of the brush she was holding skimmed the side of her hair, leaving white paint behind.

"You think you're tired?" Ford said as he reached up to pull the paint from her hair. "I could barely sleep last night with the way you were snoring so loud."

Her mouth dropped open then she caught the way his lips curved into one of those tiny flirty grins she loved. "That wasn't me. That was the donkey."

"Yeah, sure it was," he said, pulling her in for a hug as he teased her.

One of the French doors swung open, and she jumped out of the way, and out of Ford's arms, so she didn't get hit with the wet paint. "This door doesn't want to stay shut."

Ford nodded. "That's one of the biggest issues you're gonna have with an old house like this—nothing's really level anymore. Old houses sink and shift and move over the years, and things just get out of whack."

She knew a little something about getting out of whack. That was pretty much how she'd describe her life the last few months. "Does it matter if things aren't level?"

Ford shrugged. "The best answer is…sometimes."

"How is that the *best* answer?"

"If you're replacing trim around a door or window and it's off a few degrees, cosmetically it can matter if you look hard enough, but structurally, it won't make a difference. Putting those cabinet doors back on—having them level affects the way they swing and if they stay closed. That's one of the best things about keeping those original cabinet bases. Basically, you just take each situation as it comes and deal with it individually."

"I'll trust you on this. I feel like that's how I'm taking everything with this house—and my new life—one situation at a time." She offered him a small smile. "And I'm *levelheaded* enough to make up for any *level issues* in my house."

"I don't know. That joke was pretty *out of whack*."

"Oh, boo."

He pulled her to him again and leaned in to nuzzle her neck. "I don't know that you're *that* levelheaded."

"Oh, no? That's because you haven't seen that my spice rack is organized alphabetically, or that I've made a spreadsheet of my Amazon purchases to keep track of expenses for this crazy new house."

"Yeah, but you still *bought* this crazy new house."

"True."

"And you're with me. Which takes a certain kind of craziness and no degree of levelheadedness."

"Yes, also true." She hummed out a little sigh of pleasure as he kissed the spot right under her ear. "You're *making* me crazy by kissing me like that."

"Good," he said, slipping his hand under the straps of her bra and tank top then drawing them down her shoulder so he could kiss the bare skin beneath them. "Now that we've got that settled, I can focus on the real matter at hand, like giving your body the attention it deserves."

She let out a nervous giggle as heat swept up her back. "I don't know how to respond when you say things like that."

"What do you mean?"

She lowered her chin to her chest. "You just said that super sexy thing about giving attention to my body, and I guess I'm just not used to men giving me any attention at all."

Ford lifted her chin, so she was looking at him. "I wish you could see yourself through my eyes.

I don't know who hurt you or made you feel like you were less than, but it breaks my heart to hear you say things like that. And makes me even more determined to show you just amazing you, *and* your gorgeous body, are."

Ford took two steps forward, pinning her up against the wall of her new office. Raising her arms above her head, he held them there with one hand while he skimmed the other down her waist and over her thighs to tease the ragged edges of her cutoff jean shorts.

He laid hot kisses along the inside of her arm then released her hands long enough to peel her tank top over her head and toss it behind him. Her bra hit the floor next.

With her back still against the wall, she gasped as he circled one taut pebbled nipple with his tongue before sucking it between his lips. His teeth grazed the nub, sending heat surging to her core.

He unsnapped the top button of her shorts and slid the zipper down. Skimming his hand over the lacy edge of her panties, he teased her before slipping his hand inside.

She pressed her hands against the wall, pressing into him with wanton need. She hadn't told him how inexperienced she was with men. The weekend they'd spent together, she'd been pretending to be someone else, someone who knew more, who *did* more. He'd brought something out in her, some brazen side that was showing up again now as she stood with her back against the wall, her breasts bare, as she arched into him.

Her head fell back as he discovered her perfect

spot. Then his mouth was on hers, swallowing the air from her lungs, as he kissed her with hungry desire. He stroked and teased, finding the exact pressure, the precise friction, drawing her up and up until she cried out as pleasure roared through her.

Gripping his arms, she pressed her head against his shoulder and tried to catch her breath. A movement out the window caught her eye. "Oh no," she whispered. "It can't be."

"What's wrong?"

She pushed him away and scrambled for her bra. *How did it get all the way over here?* "We've got visitors."

"Ah hell," he said, grinning as he grabbed her shirt and passed it to her. "They can't be any worse than a visit from a miniature donkey with Cheetos dust on her cheeks." He looked out the window and frowned at the middle-aged couple who had parked and were getting out of a blue minivan.

Her voice came out muffled as she struggled to get her shirt on over her head. "Those are my parents."

CHAPTER NINETEEN

ELIZABETH TUGGED HER tank top around her middle as Thor and Dixie raced toward the door. What the heck were her parents doing here?

"Your *parents*?" Ford whispered, as if they could hear him from the driveway. "Did you know they were coming?"

She raised her eyebrows at him. "Do you think we would be in this state if I knew my parents were going to arrive any minute?"

He gave a quick glance down at himself. "Shit. I need a minute to…uh…settle down."

"Go upstairs," she said, smoothing her hair as she heard their footfalls on the porch steps. "Quick. I'll stall them."

He called for Dixie as he ran up the stairs. Vera, who must have heard the panic in their voices, raced up after him.

A knock sounded, then her mother pushed open the door and stepped inside. "Yoo hoo! Bitsy. Surprise!"

"Mom," Elizabeth called, hurrying toward her mother and stepping into the woman's embrace. Inhaling the scent of her mom, she hugged her tight.

She hadn't expected to see her, but she was happy she was here.

Her stepdad, on the other hand, she'd have to wait to see his reaction. She'd been doing the books for his business for years, and he hadn't been happy with her decision to move away. She was still going to be working for him—remotely—but he liked having her close where he could control everything she did.

"Stan," she said, forcing a smile as she gave him a quick hug. "What are you guys doing here?"

"Your cousins told us they'd been here, and they reported some troubling issues," her mother said, sweeping into the house and toward the kitchen. "They were right about this place being in quite the state of disrepair." She swept her fingers over the countertop then frowned as she flicked the dust away from the tips. She planted a hand on her hip. "They *even* said you had a boyfriend."

"Is that true, Bitsy?" Stan asked. "*Do* you have a boyfriend? Is he the reason you bought this rundown farm and quit your job with us?"

"First of all, I *didn't* quit my job with you. I'm still working for you. I'm just doing it remotely. And I promised to spend at least a full day in the office each quarter."

"But what about this…" Her mother stopped speaking, and her mouth dropped open as she stared at something behind Elizabeth. "…man?" she finally managed to whisper.

Elizabeth turned around, and saw Ford descend the last few stairs and step into the room. She'd been with him the last several days, but now she looked at him through her mother's eyes.

And Ford Lassiter was quite something to look at. The man was beyond handsome. He *defined* rugged good looks.

He had on a light blue T-shirt that brought out the gorgeous blue of his eyes and hugged his broad muscular chest. The sleeves fit tight around his biceps, emphasizing the sizable muscles, and his arms were tanned from the sun. He wore faded jeans and square-toed cowboy boots that slid along the wood floor as he sauntered toward them.

His dirty-blond hair was just a little too long, and he had the perfect amount of scruff along his chiseled jaw. He looked like a cross between Chris Hemsworth and Scott Eastwood.

Elizabeth swallowed, her mouth suddenly going dry. Because three minutes ago, this ridiculously hot cowboy had taken her to O-Town against that newly painted wall behind him.

"Mom. Stan. This is Ford Lassiter." She tilted her head from him to her parents. "Ford, this is my mom, Kathy, and my stepdad, Stan."

"Nice to meet you, Kathy." Ford offered her his hand and one of his grins that exuded charm.

"Please, call me Kat," she said.

"Your family loves nicknames," Ford said softly before reaching out to shake her stepdad's hand.

Stan frowned as he let go of Ford's hand. "You the contractor? Because this place has got some serious issues."

"Nice to meet you. I *am* the contractor," Ford said as he stepped back and slung his arm around Elizabeth's shoulder. "And I'm *also* the boyfriend."

"*You're* Bitsy's boyfriend?" her mother sputtered.

"I am," Ford assured her.

Elizabeth grinned up at him, her heart so full, it ached in her chest.

Kat blinked as she looked from Elizabeth to Ford then back to her daughter again. "But how? When?"

"We met at Brody and Elle's wedding," Elizabeth told her. At least that part was true. She felt kind of bad fibbing to her mother about her relationship with Ford. But dangit, her mom didn't have to act *so* shocked that she could be dating a cute cowboy.

"So, he *is* the reason you bought this dump and deserted your mother and me," Stan said.

"No, I bought this house because I wanted a change. I wanted something different in my life." She didn't think she should mention the part about giving her dog a better life. She somehow didn't think her parents would understand that. "And I don't think it *is* a dump. I love it."

"Are you kidding me?" Stan sneered as he gazed around the room. "This place is probably full of asbestos. Have you had it checked for mold?"

Her mother finally took her eyes off Ford and grimaced as she looked around. "It *is* a bit rustic, Bitsy. I mean, look at those cabinets. They're ancient."

Elizabeth's heart sank. She'd been getting ready to brag about all the work they'd done in the kitchen. "They *are* ancient, Mom. That's what gives them their charm. But we just gave them all a fresh coat of paint. Don't you love the pretty white and the navy blue? Wait until you see them with the new white quartz countertops. They've got this gorgeous vein of blueish-gray running through them that will pull this all together."

"Yes, I guess," Kat conceded. "But that refrigerator looks like it's from the nineteen-seventies."

"It probably is," Ford said. "But all new appliances are being delivered this afternoon."

"Thank goodness," Elizabeth's mom said. "But what about these floors? They look unfinished, and there is dust everywhere."

Elizabeth was so excited about all the renovations, and Ford had made her see all the possibilities of this house. But now she saw the house through her mother's eyes, and as she often did around her parents, she started to doubt herself and her decision-making abilities.

"The floors *are* unfinished," Ford explained. "And there's so much dust because we had to sand them down. But once we seal them, they're going to look amazing."

"I don't see it," Stan said, opening and closing one of the kitchen cabinets. "Isn't anything level in this place?"

Ford squeezed her shoulder. Elizabeth wished she could hold his hand, but instead she reached up and twined two of her fingers through his side belt loop as she prayed for patience.

"Would you grab the food from the car, Stan?" Kat asked then turned to smile at Elizabeth and Ford as her husband headed out the door. "I hope you're hungry. I made a lasagna and a big salad. And I had Stan stop so we could grab a loaf of that French bread from the bakery you like over on Fourth Avenue."

"Wow. Thanks, Mom." It touched her that her mother had done something so thoughtful for *her*.

"Mark my words," Kat said, pointing to a spot on the counter for Stan to set the cardboard box and the cooler he'd just carried in. "You won't find bread like that up here in *this* small town."

Stan laughed. "We drove through your Woodland Hills. What's the population here? Twenty-seven people?"

The population was actually around twelve hundred, but Elizabeth didn't think stating that would help her case. "I think it's an adorable town. And the people here are really wonderful." She turned to her mother. "Mom, your sister lives one town over in Creedence. And you always say how gorgeous it is up here when we come to visit."

"It is gorgeous," Kat admitted. "But like you said, to *visit*. Not to have my only daughter *move* up here."

"I'm only a few hours away, and there are two extra bedrooms upstairs. You can come stay whenever you want."

Her mom had taken the lid off the lasagna, so Elizabeth wasn't sure if it was the tantalizing scent of the food, or the new voices, but the sound of hooves clopping quickly down the stairs echoed in the mostly empty room—right before Vera came out of the stairwell and trotted to Elizabeth's side.

Kat let out a shriek and jumped behind Stan. "I can handle the dust, Bitsy. And the old cabinets and the wood floors, but you can't have embraced country life enough already that you have a dang donkey in your house."

CHAPTER TWENTY

ELIZABETH REACHED DOWN to give the donkey's neck a reassuring scratch. "It's okay, Mom. She's *not* my donkey."

This did not seem to reassure her mother. "Then why on earth would you have someone *else's* donkey in your house?"

"We're just watching her for a friend," Elizabeth explained. "My new neighbor actually."

"What kind of new neighbor asks you to watch their donkey?" Stan asked, taking a step back and pushing into Kat as Vera tentatively approached them.

"One who broke her hip and needed help," Ford said. "We take care of each other up here."

"And she's very sweet," Elizabeth said. "And really soft. You can pet her."

Vera sniffed at Kat's leg then pulled back her lips, offering Kat one of her smiles as she looked up at her.

"She is kind of cute." Kat cautiously reached out and patted the donkey's head. Vera rubbed her forehead against Kat's palm, and Kat let out a little laugh.

"See?" Elizabeth said. "She likes you."

"Donkeys belong in the barn." Stan reached to swat Vara away from them, and she snapped her teeth at his hand. "Did you see that? This thing tried to bite me."

She wasn't the only one who wanted to snap at him. "Sorry Stan. She doesn't really like men," Elizabeth explained.

Vera trotted over to Ford and nuzzled his legs like a cat would. A very large cat.

Elizabeth shrugged as she walked into the kitchen and grabbed some paper plates for lunch. "Except for Ford. She's apparently already fallen in love with him."

Her mom leaned closer and lowered her voice as she unloaded the box of food. "I can imagine he has that effect on most women."

She let out a nervous giggle. One that her mother caught, and Kat shot her a questioning look. Elizabeth busied herself with collecting cups and plastic cutlery.

Her mother was right, Ford *did* have that effect on most women, and Vera wasn't the only one who had already fallen for the cute cowboy.

Kat had pulled out all the stops for lunch, and had brought not only bread, lasagna, and salad, but also a chocolate cake and a tub of several dozen of Elizabeth's favorite homemade refrigerator oatmeal cookies.

After lunch, Elizabeth and Ford gave her parents a

tour of the house and property and showed them all the work they'd done and the plans they had.

"We had a lot of help from friends and neighbors this weekend," Ford explained. "So, we're much further along than I thought we would be at this point. We really just need to seal the floors then she can start moving her stuff in."

"If that's the case, then you should just ride back to Denver with us this afternoon and spend the next few days working on packing up the rest of your apartment," Kat suggested. "I can take a day off and help you shop for whatever else you need up here. Then we can get your apartment cleaned and load the U-Haul for you to drive back on Thursday, and you won't have to mess with trying to tow your car back up the pass."

"That's not a bad idea," Elizabeth told her. "I'm supposed to be out of my apartment by the middle of next week anyway. And it would be easier to not have to worry about my car."

"Now, wait a minute," Stan said. "We don't need to rush into anything. There's still time to back out of this money pit."

Elizabeth sighed. "No, there isn't. I've already closed on the house. It's mine." She looked at Ford, a little surprised at how much she was already counting on his opinions. "What do you think?"

"Seems smart. I can certainly handle the appliance delivery. And I can seal the floors tonight and tomorrow, then it'll have plenty of time to dry before you start bringing furniture in. If you came back on Thursday, we could have you all moved in and set up by the weekend."

"Sounds like we've got a plan then." Elizabeth knew she'd have to go back down the mountain to finish cleaning out her apartment, and there were several things she wanted to shop for that would be easier to do in the city. But if she left that afternoon and had her bed and furniture with her when she came back, then her nights of staying with Ford, and sleeping in his bed, would be over.

The next night, Ford climbed into bed, surprised by how much he already missed Elizabeth. Sure, they'd texted and had a quick call the night before, and for goodness sakes, she'd only been gone for a day and a half, but her absence was noticed. He hadn't slept well the night before, tossed and turned, and found himself reaching for her in the night.

Dixie had sprawled out on the now empty side of his bed, and Vera was curled up next to the dog, but neither animal was consolation for the woman who had warmed the space the last several days.

His muscles hurt and he'd taken a hot shower, hoping it would help him sleep. He'd made great progress at the house, throwing himself into the work as he tried not to think about the woman who he'd gotten used to working alongside him. He'd sealed the main floor the night before and it looked amazing when he'd come in that morning. He'd finished the wall in the master bedroom and sealed the upstairs floors before he'd left for the day.

He'd read the same page of his book for the third time because he couldn't keep his mind focused when his phone buzzed with a message, and he chastised himself for how fast he reached for it.

He had it bad for this woman. And that thought terrified him.

But it didn't stop his heart from pounding as he saw her name on the screen and tapped her message.

"You still up?"

"Yep," he typed back.

"Did you screw anything today?"

He laughed out loud. "Tons of things," he typed then paused with his fingers over the letters. Then he finished the message. "But not the one I wanted to."

The little dots flashed to show she was typing. Then they disappeared. Then they showed up again.

Had his message been too much?

Just type something already.

Finally, a message popped in, and he chuckled as he read it.

"I was trying to sound cute and funny when I said that. But then when you texted back, I remembered that I'm terrible at flirty talk and had no idea how to respond. And now I've just made it awkward so I'm going to cover my head with a pillow and go to bed."

He sent her a laughing emoji then said, "Don't go. Tell me about your day."

"It was good and bad. Good morning shopping with my mom. Found some fun stuff for the house. Bad day listening to my stepdad find a million ways to give me a hard time and make me doubt my decision to buy the house."

Ford's chest tightened. That damn Stan. Why

couldn't he leave her alone? "Do you doubt your decision?" he typed as he couldn't help but wonder if some of the things he'd been doing for her were in hopes of convincing her that she *had* made the right choice in buying the house.

"No. Not really. I mean sometimes. It is a big commitment."

He tried to think of the words to assure her that it was still a good decision. But before he could type anything, another message came in from her.

"But I'm still glad I did it. And I think it will be worth it."

Whew.

"You doing okay now?" he typed thinking the sooner she got back up the mountain and away from Stan's negative noise, the better.

"Yes. Just hot. And sweaty. Dirty from packing all day. Getting ready to take a shower."

He grinned. "Wish I was there."

"Me too. My shower is pretty lonely here."

"Wishing Vera were there to pass you the soap?"

"Exactly," her message read followed by the laughing emoji. The bubble of dots appeared again then disappeared then a new message popped up. "Hey, if I Face-Timed you, would you answer?"

"Depends. What are you wearing?"

"A slinky negligee." Her message was followed with three flame emojis.

He didn't wait for her. He pushed the Face-Time button on his screen.

She was laughing when she answered.

"Somehow that's not what I pictured when you said slinky negligee," he said, raising an eyebrow at her bulky green Colorado State University hoodie and pajama shorts. But a grin was tugging at his lips both from seeing her face and hearing her laughter.

She offered him a shy smile. "Are you disappointed?"

"Not a bit. You still look beautiful."

Pink colored her cheeks, and she let out one of those cute giggles he loved. "Hardly," she said, tugging on one of the cinnamon roll-looking buns she had her hair tied into on either side of her neck. "*You* look beautiful," she told him. "And from this angle, you look like you're naked." She blushed again after she said it.

He looked down at his bare chest and realized the blankets were pulled up over his shorts. "Maybe I am."

"Oh yeah? I can also see the book on your lap, so it can't be that wild of a night if you're reading the Farmer's Almanac."

"Hey, I'll have you know that I've got not one, but *two* females in my bed with me right now. That seems pretty wild." He turned the phone and heard her peals of laughter as he panned over Dixie and Vera curled together on his pillow.

At the sound of her laughter, Vera stood up and scrambled into his lap, sticking her long tongue out as she licked the screen of the phone.

Around the donkey's tongue, Ford saw Elizabeth laughing so hard, she fell off her bed.

Yep. Pretty wild night around here.

And surprisingly, he loved it.

The next morning, he arrived at the house at the same time as the UPS man and helped him carry several boxes of Elizabeth's purchases inside. He piled them in her office, figuring she could open them when she got back. He had no idea what all she'd ordered, but the window seat cushions and several pink pillows she'd told him about were delivered in clear plastic bags.

He stared down at the thick floral-printed cushions and grinned as an idea came to him. He grabbed the rest of the pillows and the can of pink paint and carried it all up to the attic. Looking around at all the boxes of books, he wasn't sure where to start, but he knew who would.

He pulled out his phone and scrolled through his contacts.

Maisie answered after the first ring. "Hey Ford. What's up?"

"Elizabeth is still in Denver, and I'm standing in the attic room contemplating a surprise for her. But I need some help. Any chance you have some time to help me make a book-lover's dream come true?"

She gave a quick gasp then he could hear the smile in her voice. "I'll be there in fifteen minutes."

He opened the windows, letting out the stuffy air then went back downstairs for brushes, tarps, and a ladder. He'd pushed all the boxes to the center of the room and had just got everything set up to paint when Maisie pulled up to the house.

"Come on up," he yelled out the window.

She waved up at him and then a minute later, arrived breathless at the top of the attic stairs. "I'm so excited you asked me to help. When Elizabeth showed me this secret room, she told me everything she wanted to do up here, so I already have a great picture in my head of what we need to do."

"Perfect. Because all I know is that she wanted the walls painted pink and those cushions in the window seat." He nodded to the pile of pillows. "I can get the painting done if you're willing to dust the bookshelves and start organizing the books."

She rubbed her hands together with barely suppressed glee. "I can't wait."

The large window seat was the centerpiece of the room, and most of the rounded walls were taken up with bookcases, so there wasn't a lot to paint. Ford considered giving the white bookcases a fresh coat, but they were still in good condition and the color had just a bit of an antique look to it that he wasn't sure he could match.

There was a door at the back of the room that led into the larger space of the attic that sat over the rest of the house, and it still held quite a few things from the past owners.

"Oh my gosh, this is like a collection of cool treasures and amazing antiques up here," Maisie said, peering around the larger part of the attic. "Elizabeth is going to have a blast going through all this stuff."

Ford grinned. "I'm sure she'd be happy to have you help her."

"Really?" Maisie pushed her glasses up her nose. "I would love that."

"There's plenty of stuff in the library room that I don't think we'll need, so I figured we'd just bring it in here, and if Elizabeth wants to use it later, she can."

"I was thinking the same thing. I doubt she's going to want to put every single book back on the shelves, plus she's going to have her own books she'll want to put up. I thought I would just go through the boxes and curate out the classics and some of the ones that I think she'll love, then we can store the rest for later. Do you think she'd be okay if I brought in some of these treasures?" She pointed to a birdcage in the corner and an open box of old dishes. "That birdcage would look so neat with a candle inside of it, and I think I can see a teapot and cups in that box of dishes."

"Knock yourself out," Ford told her. "This stuff all belonged to Frank and Ida, so it's not like you're snooping in Elizabeth's stuff. And I'm sure she wouldn't care anyway."

"I've already got so many cute ideas. And I may run home at lunch and grab a few things that I have that would be perfect in this space." She pulled back the edge of a rolled-up rug that was encased in plastic and leaning against one wall and let out an excited squeal. "Oh my gosh, this rug is mint green and looks like it has pink roses on it. If it's the right size, it would be so pretty in the library room."

"We can take it down and roll it out in the backyard. If it looks okay, we can give it a good shaking then bring it back up." He hefted the rug onto his shoulder, not mentioning that another reason he wanted to unroll it outside was in case they found a nest of mice or mice droppings inside.

But they found the rug to be in great shape when

they unrolled it in the backyard, and Maisie let out another excited squeal.

"This is going to be perfect," she said. "When I go home at lunch, I'll also bring back my vacuum and a little steam cleaner I have. That'll get the musty scent out of it, and it will be dry before Elizabeth gets home tomorrow."

They set to work, Ford painting while Maisie unpacked and shelved books. He moved boxes out of the room and retrieved whatever he and Maisie thought would work in the library.

After lunch, Maisie brought back a few dried flower creations, some scented candles, and several cute bookish decorations like a sign that read, "So many books, so little time," a small teal throw pillow that said, "Just One More Chapter," and a little sign to hang on the doorknob that read, "Come back later—I'm reading".

Later that afternoon, after it had been vacuumed and steam-cleaned, he moved the rug back in, then they unwrapped the new cushions and pillows and placed them in the window seat.

Maisie let out a wistful sigh as she looked around the room, now full of feminine pink and white accents, classic books, and antique décor. "She's going to absolutely love it."

Ford couldn't hold back the grin. He thought so too.

Ford was thrilled when he got a call that same afternoon that the countertops were finished and ready to be installed. He called in a favor to a plumbing friend and stayed late so they could finish everything in the kitchen that night.

But the kitchen and the attic reading nook weren't the only surprises Ford had in store for Elizabeth's return the next day.

He should have been tired after the day spent transforming the reading nook and helping to finish the kitchen, but instead of going to bed, he stayed at her house and worked on another idea he'd had. Only this one wasn't so much for Elizabeth. It was more for Thor.

She had told him several times that she wanted to give her dog a better life. So, when he'd found a stack of lumber in the barn and a new roll of white picket fencing, he couldn't resist the idea of making Thor a doghouse and replacing the old fencing around the front yard with new.

Without all the weeds choking the yard, he was surprised to see quite a bit of green lawn. And with the afternoon thunderstorms they'd been having the past few days, there was even evidence of some new grass coming up. The gardening crew had cut away the dead branches that hid the view of the river, so he'd grabbed a couple of plastic Adirondack chairs he'd seen at the hardware store the day before to put in the backyard.

He'd heard some doubt in her voice the last few times he'd talked to Elizabeth about whether she'd made the right decision to buy this house. He was sure Stan and Kat had been filling her head with all sorts of reasons why this move was a terrible idea.

But he was proud of Elizabeth for making this decision. Even if the house did have some issues, it still had good bones. And she had stepped out of her comfort zone and done something for herself. Which he was coming to realize, she didn't often do. The more he learned about her, the more he realized she spent most of her time putting others before herself. Which was even more reason why he wanted to give her these surprises.

When Elizabeth got home tomorrow, she would drive up to see a new white picket fence around the yard, a freshly painted doghouse for Thor, and the new chairs set up in the back to take in the view of the river. And he couldn't wait to see her face when she walked up the stairs to her new attic reading nook. He felt like he was giving her a Christmas morning and a birthday celebration all wrapped up in one.

The next morning, Elizabeth showered and finished packing her suitcase. She was anxious to get on the road and back to her house. And to Ford.

She wasn't anxious about the drive though. Stan had convinced her to rent the bigger U-Haul truck, even though she'd never driven anything that size, let alone over a mountain pass. But these last few weeks had been full of moments when she'd found herself doing one brave thing at a time, and driving this truck was just going to be one more thing she'd have to find the courage to do.

Because the reward up the mountain was worth it.

Kat had made coffee, but both she and Stan had hugged Elizabeth earlier and then headed to work. Elizabeth filled a travel mug with the last of the coffee, stirred in some creamer then called for Thor. She'd told Ford she planned to be on the road by nine and it was only a few minutes past the hour.

She opened the front door, and Thor went racing out ahead of her, sprinting across the lawn to where a handsome cowboy leaned against the side of the U-Haul truck.

CHAPTER TWENTY-ONE

ELIZABETH COULDN'T BELIEVE her eyes. She hurried after the dog, just as excited as Thor, but trying not to sprint toward him, throw herself into his arms, and lick his face as her dog was doing. "Oh my gosh. Ford. What are you doing here?"

He shrugged as if it were no big deal that he'd driven over two hours to see her. "We were all worried about you driving this truck up the pass, and Gramps has been wanting to do a Costco run anyway, so Chevy drove us down, and dropped me off so I could drive up the mountain with you. If you're set on driving, I'm happy to just ride along too. But I thought you might at least want the company."

She threw her arms around his neck and hugged him tight. "I can't believe it. I'm terrified of driving this thing, but I was just trying to work up the courage to do it. And now you're here, and…I don't have to…and oh gosh…you just made me so happy." She blinked back the tears welling in her eyes.

"Hey now, I didn't mean to make you cry," he said, wiping a lone tear from her cheek.

"They're good tears. Happy tears. So incredibly

thankful tears." She beamed up at him, unable to control the smile spreading across her face. "I still can't believe you're here. I just want to pinch myself to make sure you're real."

"I'll do you one better," he said then leaned down to capture her lips in a kiss that sent molten heat surging through her veins.

She wasn't sure he was really making his point, because finding a hot cowboy outside of her parents' house and then having him kiss her thoroughly certainly felt like she had to be dreaming.

The drive up the mountain took close to three hours. Elizabeth had decided to face down one more of her fears and drive the truck herself. Having Ford by her side gave her the extra confidence she needed, and she was proud of herself for taking the wheel and tackling the drive.

Even though the trip was longer than usual, the time flew by as Elizabeth filled Ford in on all that had been happening the past few days and listened as he gave her the latest updates on the house.

The cab of the truck was quieter without Dixie and Vera, but Ford had told her he'd left the golden and the donkey at home with Dodge.

"He made a few wise cracks about being put on donkey duty, but Dodge is a sucker for any animal," Ford told her. "He found a hurt porcupine once when we were kids—it had been hit by a car—and he convinced Gramps to put it in the truck and take it to the vet. He wanted to keep the thing as a pet when it got better."

"Oh no. I am a city girl, but I wouldn't think a porcupine would make a very good pet."

"No, it wouldn't."

"But, in his defense, at least it would be better than a skunk."

Ford laughed. "I love the way you see the world."

"I love hearing stories about you and your brothers," she said. "Tell me some more. What was Ford Lassiter like as a kid?"

"Pretty much the same as I am now. A broody loner who takes on too much responsibility for his brothers, who is occasionally witty, but usually just seems annoyed and angry at the world."

She huffed out a laugh. "Wow. Is that really how you see yourself?"

He shrugged. "I'm not sure why that got a laugh from you, but yeah, I guess. Why? How do you see me?"

"As a caring, kind, thoughtful guy who takes his time making decisions by thinking through every possibility. I see you as a caretaker of your brothers and your grandfather, not in the way that you necessarily *do* things for them, but that you watch out for them. And I think you are *often* witty. You make *me* laugh all the time."

"You're an exception. And I think you're just easily entertained, because you find the good and the fun in the world."

She blinked. "Gosh, I've never thought of myself that way."

"How do you see yourself?"

She kept her eyes on the road to avoid looking at him. "As an awkward introvert who is afraid to make decisions, who has no self-control when it comes to pizza or ice cream, who has a nerdy job and a boring life, and who tries to pretend that she's brave but still gets the nervous giggles when she's around a certain handsome cowboy."

His expression turned thoughtful, and his voice was soft as he asked, "Really?"

She shrugged.

He picked up her hand, pulled it to his lips, and pressed a soft kiss against her knuckles. "I see you as smart, kind, and funny as hell. You are always thinking of others before yourself, and I don't think you're awkward or nerdy. I think it takes intelligence to do the work you do, and you should be proud that you're good at your job and that people trust you with one of their most treasured assets—their money. I think making a big change in your life like you've done takes guts and courage, especially when your family keeps tearing you down."

She swallowed, not sure she could trust her voice to speak. Did he really see her that way? His words filled something inside her, a hole that had gotten deeper with every boy who had teased her about her weight or about how tall she was or called her a nerd for reading books all the time. A hole that had widened with the times she'd found the courage to meet a guy she'd met online for coffee or a drink and seen the disappointment in his eyes when his gaze had traveled down her body.

"Thank you," she whispered.

"I'm not done," he said, brushing his lips over her

knuckles again and sending shivers of pleasure down her spine. "I also think you're beautiful. And I love those nervous giggles, especially when I'm the one causing them. I hate that you put your body down. So what if you love pizza and ice cream and have a few curves. I love your curves. In fact, I've spent quite a bit of time the last few days thinking about them. And when I could get my hands on them again."

She pressed her lips together to hold in one of those giggles. "I've been thinking about that too."

"Oh yeah?" His voice took on that cocky flirty tone. "Anything you want to share?"

One of those giggles escaped. She could hold her own when they were teasing each other about power tools or pizza choices, but she was in over her head when it came to exchanging banter about sexy times. The words were in her head, she had been thinking *so* many things about being with him again, it just made her feel silly saying them out loud.

She tried to think of what she felt comfortable telling him. "Um…well…I have been wondering if that bathtub in the master bathroom was big enough for two."

He grinned and teased her knuckles with his lips again. "There's only one way to find out."

Thor, who had been sitting up in the seat between them, suddenly jumped into Ford's lap to bark out the window at two deer standing in the trees by the side of the road. Ford let go of her hand so he could keep the dog from falling off the seat.

After that interruption, they stopped for a gas and snack break, and their conversation went back to discussing the house and their plans for getting everything unpacked.

Thirty minutes later, Elizabeth leaned forward as she pulled the U-Haul up to her house. She'd spent the past few days listening to her mother and stepdad tell her every reason under the sun why buying this house had been a mistake.

But, as she peered at the old Victorian farmhouse, with its new porch and side tower, and spruced up yard, her heart filled with joy and excitement.

She bounced up and down in her seat and clapped her hands as she saw the new addition to the yard. "Oh my gosh. You replaced the white picket fence. I love it."

Ford chuckled. "If you get this excited about the fence, you're gonna *really* love all the rest of the surprises I have for you."

"*All* the rest? I wasn't expecting *any* surprises at all."

He smiled and gave her a flirty wink. "I know. That's what makes it so fun to give them to you." He got out while she was collecting her purse and hurried around to open the door and offer his hand to help her out of the truck. "Do you want to see inside before we unload your stuff?"

"Yes. I'm dying to see how the floors turned out."

Ford was grinning like a kid in a candy shop as they walked into the yard. "I want to show you, *and Thor*, one thing first."

"Ohhh-kay." What the heck did he want to show her dog?

She followed him around the house then covered her mouth as she gasped at the small doghouse that sat by the back door. It was painted white and had 'THOR' stenciled in black over the door. "Oh. My. Gosh. Did you *make* this?"

Ford nodded, his grin widening even more.

"For Thor?" She shook her head and laughed at herself. "That was a silly question. Obviously, you didn't make it for *me*."

He shrugged. "Sort of. I guess I made it for both of you. You told me you wanted your dog to have a better life. What better life for a dog than a fancy doghouse where he can sleep and keep a watchful eye on the yard for any wayward deer or bunny rabbits."

Thor went racing over to investigate and sniff his new digs. Then he disappeared inside.

"Oh look," Elizabeth said, pointing to the doghouse. "He likes it. He went right in."

Ford lifted one shoulder and offered her a sheepish grin. "I may have tossed some dog treats in there before I left this morning. I wasn't taking any chances that he might not like it."

"But you were taking a pretty big chance hoping that a raccoon or skunk wouldn't have sniffed out those treats and already moved in before Thor got here."

"Yeah, I know. It was a risky move, but it was worth it."

"Yes, it was. I absolutely love it. And I guess if there had been a racoon or skunk, Dodge could have just taken it home for a pet." She laughed then turned and caught sight of the new chairs in the yard. "Wow. Where did these chairs come from? I love them, too."

"I picked them up from the hardware store. I saw you looking at them the last time we were there. And I thought they'd be perfect for sitting out here and watching the river. I was gonna get a fire pit too, but I didn't know if you'd want one that uses propane or firewood. I figured we could pick one out next time we're in town."

She loved the chairs. But what she loved even more was that he'd bought them with the idea in mind that they'd sit out here together. Like a real couple.

Her throat was thick with emotion. "This is all just so perfect. I can't believe you did this for me."

"This was no big deal," he said, but his smile showed he was pleased. "If a doghouse and a couple of chairs makes you this happy, you're going to lose your mind at the last surprise. But first, I can't wait for you to see how the floors turned out." He took her hand and led her back around to the front porch.

She wanted to cry again when he opened the door, and she stepped inside. The wood floors gleamed with the fresh coat of shiny sealant. "They're gorgeous," she said. "Are they okay to walk on?"

"Oh yeah. They're completely dry," he said, leading her into the living room. "Can you believe what a difference adding that glossy sealant made?"

"No. I can't believe any of this." She shook her head, torn between wanting to laugh and cry as she walked farther into the living room and then gasped again at the sight of the shiny new stainless-steel appliances and the gorgeous new countertops.

She squealed as she raced into the kitchen and ran her hands over the smooth counters, marveling at the beautiful bluish-gray vein that ran through the pearly white quartz. "They look amazing. I can't believe you didn't tell me the countertops were installed."

"And ruin the surprise? No way. I was blown away when they called yesterday and said they were done already. I guess they had a cancellation yesterday, so they just went ahead and got yours cut. I was staying late over here anyway, so I told them to bring 'em out. And I've got a buddy who's a plumber, so I talked him into coming over last night and we installed the sink, hooked up the dishwasher and disposal, and ran the water line for the fridge."

Her eyes widened as she stared at him. "So, it all works?"

"Yep."

"How did you get all this done? I've only been gone for two and a half days."

He shrugged. "It's a small town, and I called in a few favors. Although the plumbing cost me a bucket of chicken and a six pack of fancy IPA, but I'll add that to your tab."

"Please do." Laughing, she ran around the kitchen, touching all the appliances and opening and closing the refrigerator and oven doors. She lifted the handle at the sink and beamed at the rush of water that streamed through the new brushed nickel faucet. "I love all of it. Every. Single. Thing. I can't believe this is *my* house, and I get to live here *every* day."

She ran to him and threw her arms around his neck. "You keep acting like this was no big deal, but you doing all of this, it means everything to me. It's so beautiful. I can't thank you enough."

"You don't have to thank me. I've enjoyed seeing it all come together. It's been a fun project."

He hugged her back, but something in her chest tightened. She hadn't expected it to be finished so quickly. It had all come together so fast. But once the project was done then there would be no reason for her to hang out with and see Ford every day.

Which meant she should make hay while the sun shines. Or in this case, kiss the hell out of the cowboy while she had the chance.

His arms tightened around her as she kissed his lips. Softly at first, then with more intention. She'd missed the feel of his body against hers, the strong grip of his hands as they ran down her back and cupped her butt. He lifted her onto the countertop of the center island and her legs wrapped tightly against his waist, her desperate need for him evident in the ache in her core.

A horn honked outside as Dodge's truck pulled up out front.

"You've got to be kidding me," Ford said, his breath ragged as he pressed his forehead to hers. "What is it with us and these countertops? Every time I get you on one, we get interrupted."

"At least I still have my top on this time."

He cocked an eyebrow. "In what way does that make this any better? If my little brother would have arrived only a few minutes later, I would have had you naked, writhing, and calling out my name on this new quartz."

She swallowed. *Oh dang.* "That sounds pretty good to me. Do you want to go out and tell him to come back later?"

He laughed and kissed her again. "Yes, I do. But I won't. Because I already owe him pizza and a six-pack for coming out to help us unload this truck."

"In that case, yes, we need him to stay," she said, hopping down from the counter. "And I'm buying the pizza and beer."

"You're on," he said, heading toward the front door.

"Hey Ford," she said, grabbing his hand and pulling him back for one more kiss. "We might not have the greatest luck with these countertops, but I'm feeling good about our chances with the bathtub…"

His eyes widened then he let out a roguish laugh as he took her mouth in another sinfully delicious kiss.

CHAPTER TWENTY-TWO

ELIZABETH SMOOTHED HER hair and tried to catch her breath as Ford went to let his brother in. But when he opened the front door, it wasn't Dodge that came racing inside. Instead, it was an enthusiastic golden retriever and an excited miniature donkey who came running, and galloping, inside.

Dixie ran to Ford like she hadn't seen him in days instead of hours then she raced to Elizabeth, her furry butt wiggling like mad. But Elizabeth had her hands full with Vera, who was braying and whinnying and trying to tunnel between her legs. The donkey's ears were back, and her tail was wagging almost as hard as the dogs as she rubbed back and forth across Elizabeth's legs.

"I think they're excited to see us," Elizabeth said, trying to keep her balance and not get knocked over by the dog's and donkey's greetings.

"I'm glad to see you too," Dodge said, coming into the house and giving Elizabeth a hug. He jerked his thumb toward the little donkey. "I don't wiggle my ass for just anyone."

Elizabeth barked out a laugh that probably

sounded a little like the donkey's bray. She covered her mouth but continued to laugh hard enough that a snort slipped out. Dodge's joke might have been cheesy and maybe not snort-worthy, but she was just so happy. And after spending the last few days with her parents, Mr. and Mrs. Doom and Gloom, it felt good to laugh.

She looked over and caught Ford grinning at her. The way he was smiling, like he was actually happy, and that *she* had something to do with that happiness, had a swarm of butterflies taking off in her belly.

Over the last few days, she'd tried to convince herself she would be all right if Ford eventually left her. That taking things one day at a time with no thought to the future was okay with her. She *was* having fun. *And* having the best sex of her life.

If he left her, like he *told her* he would, she had to believe that this experience with him would still be worth it. That having her heart broken—and make no mistake, Ford walking out of her life *would* shatter her—was worth getting to spend this time with him.

Being his girlfriend, even if it was pretend, or just a ruse, felt real to her. The feelings she had were real, the sex they'd been having, the kisses, the soft touches, those were all real too. And they had to be enough.

"You ready to move into your new house?" he asked, wrapping his arm around her waist and pulling her to him.

Ignoring the creeping feeling that it was too late, that she had already fallen head over heels in love with him, she clapped her hands together and grinned up at him. "Heck, yes."

Ford backed the U-Haul up to the house, and they got started carrying things in. Moving a one-bedroom apartment into a three-bedroom house didn't take long. Most of the boxes went to the kitchen, her bedroom, or the master bath.

She followed the guys up when they carried in her bed and was thrilled that Ford had not only finished the wall but had already painted it too. Having the arched doorway brought in more light and made the space seem so much bigger. She loved it.

She and her mom had found a light gray sofa and matching loveseat at a consignment store, and they fit perfectly into the living room. She wanted to keep the original kitchen table and planned to refinish it after she got settled, so she'd bought some cute kitchen chairs to go with it and had also picked out a couple of new bar stools for the kitchen island.

Kat had insisted on getting her three matching end tables for the living room, and Elizabeth was surprised at how well they worked in the space and gave every seat a place to set a drink.

She dug through the new boxes piled in her office to find the sheets she'd ordered and got them in the washing machine while the guys put the bed frame together. She also opened the boxes with the lamps and got them set up as well.

Now that the kitchen was finished, Elizabeth was able to start unpacking and getting the space set up. She'd splurged on a new set of navy-blue dishes since the ones from her apartment had been just a mismatched set from her college days. As she unpacked, she made a list of all the things she'd still need to make her new kitchen complete.

Dodge stuck around to help Ford set up the Wi-Fi and hook up her television and a few of her smart devices. When they'd finished, Dodge followed Ford into town to return the U-Haul and they came back with a pizza, a six-pack, and a bottle of wine.

Dodge opened the pizza box, and the mouthwatering scents of garlic and pepperoni filled the room. "Hey, I heard Maisie was out here yesterday helping you with- –"

"A surprise for Elizabeth that she hasn't seen yet," Ford said, cutting off his brother's next words. "So, ix-nay on the Aisie-May discussion."

"When do I get to see this last surprise?" she asked, thankful she'd already unpacked the two wineglasses she owned as she poured sparkling Moscato into one.

Ford shrugged and offered her a roguish grin. "I know how much you're gonna love it, so maybe I'm saving it for when we're alone and you can *show* me your appreciation."

She knew he was just teasing her, but she'd just taken a sip of wine, and a half-giggle, half-hiccup bubbled out of her at his flirty jest. Lifting one shoulder in a shrug, she offered him a coy smile in return. "I was already planning to show you my *appreciation* for coming to get me this morning and driving the truck up the pass and helping me unload all this stuff. And I have *a lot* of appreciation planned."

Dodge made a sound like he was trying to retch. "Hey now. You two realize I'm still in the room, right? Save your *appreciating* each other business for when I'm gone."

"Sorry, brother." Ford chuckled but didn't seem that sorry as he slugged his brother in the arm.

"Seriously though, I can't thank you enough for helping me out today," Elizabeth told Dodge. "It was so nice of you to give up your afternoon for me."

He waved her off as he opened a bottle of beer. "Don't even mention it. My brother would never admit it, but he does a lot for Chevy and me. We're always glad when we get a chance to do something for him."

She understood that. But they weren't doing this for their brother. They were doing it for her. Guilt settled in her stomach at the reminder that she and Ford weren't really a couple, so everything his brothers were doing for him felt like a trick she was pulling on them.

Which is what she told Ford an hour later after his brother had left.

"It's not a trick or a scam," he told her. "Even if we aren't technically a real couple, we're still friends. So don't think we're pulling the wool over anyone's eyes. They would still help, even if we were just friends."

She wasn't sure if that made her feel any better.

Thankfully, the dryer in the mudroom buzzed, giving her a reason to change the subject.

"Those are the sheets," she said.

"Do you want me to help you make the bed?" he asked.

"Sure."

Then I want you to help me unmake it as we tangle up my new sheets.

He grabbed the clean laundry from the dryer while she brought up the comforter, new pillow shams, and her favorite cozy pink throw she'd had on her bed in her apartment. Even though she was creating something new, it was nice to have a few touches of the familiar.

Elizabeth fluffed the final throw pillow then stood back to admire the bed after they finished making it. "It looks great."

"Nah, it's missing one thing." Ford swooped her into his arms and carried her fireman style back to the bed. "You. Naked, and in it."

A thrill ran through her, heat and pleasure, making her nipples tighten as he yanked back the comforter and set her on the sheets. His eyes traveled over her, a devilish grin curving his lips as he noted the hardened nubs poking through the thin cotton of her tank top.

"I want to see you," he all but growled. Then in one swift movement, he stripped her running shorts down her legs and tossed them to the floor. Reaching for the hem of her shirt, he tugged it over her head and flung it somewhere behind him.

She leaned back against the pillows, feeling the heat of his gaze as he drank in the sight of her body. Using one finger, he released the clasp at the front of her bra, freeing her aching breasts and filling his hands with them. She bit back a moan as he grazed his thumb over one tightened tip.

He leaned in and laid a warm kiss along her neck, then one on her collarbone then another one even lower. His breath on her bare skin was soft. But the scrape of his whiskers against her breasts had her dropping her head back and arching up, her body craving his touch, desperate with need.

His strong hand caressed the curve of her waist then he slid his fingers under the waistband of her lacy panties and drew them slowly down her legs. The opposite of how he'd ripped her shorts off, this was a slow delicious torture as he bent his head and kissed the soft flesh of her belly then skimmed his lips across her ribs.

She parted her legs, a silent gesture of consent, then inhaled a quick gasp at the rasp of his jaw against the inner side of her thigh. His breath teased and tormented her—the whisper of it against her sensitive skin. He'd barely touched her, and she was already unraveling at the seams.

Powerless against him, she lay naked and exposed, trembling with anticipation of his touch. He was still fully clothed. He hadn't even taken off his boots.

For a moment, she felt embarrassed and wanted to pull the sheets over herself, then she took a deep breath and embraced the new courage she'd found in herself. And instead of covering her nakedness, she pulled back her shoulders and arched her back, a wanton gesture of offering more of herself to him. His eyes darkened with hunger as he accepted her offer.

The erotic sensations of his lips, his hands, his gaze, on her body had her slim grasp of control slipping.

She watched, aching with awareness of his every move, spellbound as he lavished her body with attention, touching, caressing, licking, stroking. Tingles and ripples of desire shimmered through her, and she thought she might die from the feeling.

He pulled away, and she let out a soft whimper, missing the feel of his hands on her. But every nerve in her body heated as he tugged off his boots, ripped off his shirt, and pulled a foil packet from his pocket before shimmying out of his jeans.

He covered himself then climbed into the bed and settled between her legs. She let out a sigh at the weight of him and tunneled her fingers through his hair, pulling his mouth down to hers. His kiss was deep and demanding, and she moaned into his mouth as if drawing him deeper still.

A growl vibrated at the back of his throat as he buried himself in her, and she dropped her head back, crying out.

She was utterly at his mercy, every nerve in her body taut, the visceral need for this man almost overwhelming her. Everything else fell away—the only thing that mattered was her and Ford and the passion that burned between them. The intensity heightened, her fevered nerve endings begging for release as the sensations rushed through her, seizing her muscles, then she cried out once again, gripping his shoulders as the waves of pleasure coursed through her.

His hold on her tightened and his teeth grazed her shoulder as he shuddered and tensed, growling out his own release. Then he pulled back, bracing himself on his arms above her as he stared down at her. His gaze was soft, loving, as he brushed her hair from her forehead.

At least she'd *thought* it was loving. So much so, that when he whispered, "You're so beautiful," she whispered back, "I love you."

CHAPTER TWENTY-THREE

ELIZABETH KNEW IMMEDIATELY she'd made a mistake.

She knew it by the way Ford's eyes had widened then his whole expression changed. His lips tightened then his body tensed as his gaze shifted away from hers. He collapsed onto the bed next to her but didn't drag her next to him as he usually did.

Instead, he scrubbed his hand through his hair and blew out a weighty sigh.

"I'm sorry," she said, pushing up on her elbow and rolling toward him. "Forget I said that. *Please* forget I said that."

"I can't forget it," he said softly then pushed off the bed and grabbed his pants off the floor. "I have to go."

She pulled the sheet up to cover herself. "Go? What do you mean *go*?"

"I mean I can't do this. This is too much." He shoved his legs into his pants and yanked on his T-shirt. "We were fooling ourselves that we thought we could keep this casual."

"No, I can. I'm sorry. We're pretending to be in a

relationship anyway, so just pretend that I didn't say that."

"I can't. I told you that I was no good at relationships. Apparently even fake ones." Even as he was breaking her heart, his face held an anguished expression. "I need to go. And you need to focus on all that stuff you said you wanted—on the new life you're trying to start."

"But *you* were one of those things I wanted."

"I know. I'm sorry. I tried to warn you."

She nodded and tried to keep her voice from shaking. "You did. And I accepted the risk. I told you I wasn't asking for promises. I knew what I was getting into." She had known from the start that he would eventually leave her. She wasn't the kind of girl that guys stuck around for. So, this shouldn't be that big of a surprise. But it still cut her to the core.

His voice was husky with emotion. "I wish I were different."

"You're just being you." Her gaze cut to a spot on the wall behind him. She couldn't look him in the eye. "So, if you have to go, I understand. And I'll be okay." She lifted one shoulder in a small shrug. "And now at least I know what real love feels like."

He punched his fist against the side of his leg. "I knew this would happen. I knew I would hurt you. That's why I have to leave, before I make things even worse."

How could this get any worse? He had just had mind-blowing sex with her then he'd pulled on his pants and was walking away.

"I'm not trying to completely desert you," he said. "I'll still help finish the house. But if I go now, if I stop this thing between us, then maybe we still have a chance of being friends. I swear, I still want us to be friends."

"Sure, Ford. We can still be friends." She swallowed at the painful lump in her throat and lifted her chin as she tried to find the courage to let him go. "I just need some time to get over being in love with you."

Ford slammed his fist against the dashboard as he tore out of Elizabeth's driveway.

I'm such an asshole.

What the hell had he just done?

He'd just destroyed the one person who he'd never wanted to hurt. And he knew he'd shattered her. He'd seen it in her eyes. Elizabeth already felt like she wasn't good enough. And now he was the one who would add to that doubt about herself and how amazing she really was.

I'm such an asshole.

He'd tried to warn her. He'd told her he would hurt her. And she'd just accepted it and told him she understood.

Dixie whined as she crawled across the seat and laid her head against his shoulder. He wrapped his arm around the dog's shoulders and hugged her to him. "Why do I do this?" he asked the dog.

He'd had a chance to have everything he'd ever wanted, and he just threw it away.

He was already regretting it, wishing he could take it all back. If he had just kept his damn mouth shut, he would still be in her bed.

And he wouldn't have broken her heart.

I'm such an asshole.

Thor jumped up on the bed and pawed at Elizabeth's arm, the signal that he needed to go outside. It had been hours since Ford had walked out of the room, but she hadn't moved. She'd just pulled the covers up and curled into a ball then laid there and relived every moment of the last few hours. Of the last few days.

Stupid.

Why had she told him she loved him? She knew it would freak him out.

She let out a heavy sigh and forced herself to get out of bed. She found a pair of pajama pants and a tank top to put on. One of Ford's flannel shirts was tossed over a ladder in the corner of her room—he must've taken it off when he was working then forgotten about it. Elizabeth picked it up and held it to her face, inhaling the scent of him. She held back a sob as she pulled it on over her pajamas, wrapping it around herself and imagining it was Ford's arms circling her instead of just his shirt.

Still feeling chilled, she dragged the cozy pink throw from the end of the bed and wrapped it around her shoulders as well as she trudged downstairs and into the kitchen. She poured a glass of water from the tap then took a long drink, trying to cool the ache in her throat.

She opened the refrigerator and stared inside but nothing looked good. And nothing could quell the real hunger she was feeling.

She followed the dog and donkey outside and stood barefoot in the yard, looking up at the sky. The scent of rain was in the air, and she could feel the weight of a storm brewing. The sky lit with a flash of lightning and thunder rumbled a few seconds later. Stormy was a good way to describe how she was feeling. Her thoughts were heavy with the sadness of impending rain, but her stomach was a mixture of rage and chaos. She was sad, but also mad at herself for ruining everything with Ford. Why hadn't she just kept her big mouth shut?

Everything had been going so well, then she blew it. She had to have come across as too anxious, too eager. Of course, she'd scared Ford away.

In her heart, she knew she never really deserved a man like him anyway. He was too good-looking, too kind, too *everything*. And so far out of her league that they weren't even playing in the same game.

But he *had* cared about her. She had to believe that. Didn't she? If he didn't care, then he wouldn't have been so freaked out by her declaration of love.

As she stared into the sky, a flash of movement caught her eye, and she sucked in a breath at the shooting star streaking across the inky space. Pressing her lips together, she tried not to cry as tears filled her eyes and she held the shooting star pendant around her neck.

She had tried so damn hard to be brave. To step out of her box and do one brave thing. Hell, she had done numerous brave things over the last month. All starting with meeting Ford and the first time she got into his truck. Since that moment, she'd broken her lease, changed her job, culled half her belongings, bought this farmhouse, took on the care of a miniature donkey, and shared the bed of the hottest cowboy she'd ever seen.

And she hadn't just shared Ford's bed, she'd shared his life. For the briefest of moments, he'd let her into his thoughts, his family, his world.

She *had* been brave.

A drop of rain hit her cheek, and she tilted her face to the sky, letting the tiny spatters of moisture fall onto her skin.

Maybe instead of thinking the rain symbolized sadness, she could try to think of it as a new beginning, a feeling of being washed clean then offered a fresh start. Regardless of what happened with Ford, she *had* moved to Woodland Hills. She'd unloaded all her things into her new house. This *was* her life now. She needed to make the best of it. With or *without* Ford Lassiter's presence in it.

The rain fell harder, and she called for Thor and Vera as she dashed inside. Going through the motions, she gave them each food and fresh water, but still didn't feel like eating anything herself.

Dodge's work gloves sat on the edge of the counter, and she suddenly remembered him saying Maisie had been here the day before. Ford had said she'd helped him with the big surprise. But he'd never gotten a chance to tell her what the big surprise was.

She looked for something that stood out as she wandered aimlessly around the main level, but nothing struck her as being surprise worthy.

Back upstairs, she drifted through the empty spare rooms. She could call Maisie and just ask her what the surprise was. But then she might have to explain why Ford hadn't shown it to her himself—and she wasn't ready to do that. Not yet.

Back in the hallway, she noticed that the door to the attic room was slightly ajar, and a small sign that said, "Come back later—I'm reading" hung from the doorknob.

She opened the door and flipped on the light switch as she peered up the stairs. Pulling the throw tighter around her shoulders, she climbed the stairs to the attic room.

Or to what *used to be* the attic room.

Her mouth hung open as she stared at the gorgeous transformation. Then she let out the sob she'd been fighting to keep trapped in her throat as she sunk onto the window seat. Tears fell freely down her cheeks as she gazed around the room at the freshly painted pink walls, the old books neatly stacked on the shelves, the pretty candles and antique decorations that had been so thoughtfully placed.

A small white tea cart sat next to the window seat holding a cute floral tea pot with a matching cup and saucer. A mint green rug with pink roses covered the floor.

The pretty floral cushions and pillows she'd ordered fit perfectly in the window seat, and she curled onto her side and stared out the window at the farmyard in front of her. *Her* farmyard. She pulled the throw around and used it like a blanket to cover herself.

She couldn't believe Ford had done this for her.

She'd told him she'd wanted to paint the room pink. He could have done just that, and she would have been thrilled. But this was so much more. This took thought and effort, and the fact that Maisie had helped made it even more special. She could imagine the parts the librarian had helped with—the candles and the flowers artfully arranged next to the neatly stacked books. And the cute little signs and teal pillow had to be Maisie's ideas. There was no way Ford had found those.

With another sigh, she again tried to think of her situation in a new way, to force herself to think of something besides Ford. She thought, *hoped*, she had found a new friend in Maisie. She'd met several people in the community. Her house, no, her *home*, was beautiful. It was painted and styled just the way she wanted.

For the first time in her life, she had something that was just hers—that she had saved up for and purchased all on her own. Something that was more than just a bike or a new hardcover book. Something she had poured blood, sweat, and tears into, and that she had made her own.

Except, everywhere she looked, she saw traces of Ford. He had been an integral part of everything they had done to renovate the home, from the floors to the paint on the walls, to enlarging her bedroom, to helping her pick out the kitchen faucets and new cabinet hardware.

And now he was gone.

Well, not gone. He still wanted to be *friends*. Although how she was ever going to go back to being just his friend was beyond her. But maybe it could work. They had never really had a chance to be *just friends*. They had gone from zero to one hundred the first weekend they'd met.

She had told Ford everything he'd wanted to hear tonight—that they could still be friends, that she had known what she was getting into, that she understood why he was leaving, and that she would be okay.

But every bit of that was a lie.

She was *not* going to be okay. She wasn't sure she would ever be okay again.

She thought she knew what she was getting into—thought she could do a little casual sex and then easily let him go when he decided to walk away.

But she had never been more wrong about anything in her life.

She did *not* know what she was getting into. She did *not* know that she would develop such strong feelings for him…that he would break her when he left.

She didn't know that she'd fall in love with his laugh, his gentle touch, the way he brushed his fingers along her arm when he walked past her, the way he frowned at a project when he was thinking, the way he adored his dog, the respect and care he showed his grandfather, the funny growling sound he made to indicate his annoyance.

But she had.

And there wasn't a damn thing she could do about it.

She'd already fallen, and damn her big mouth—already spoken the words aloud.

Another sob escaped her, and Thor jumped up on the window seat and tried to cuddle in on the pillow next to her head. She let out another half-cry, half-laugh as Vera scrambled up too and wiggled into the space between her and the window. Both animals tried to lick the tears from her face.

She gave them each a pet, but their cuddles weren't enough to stem the sadness stealing through her. As she stared into the dark rainy night, her tears fell, and her body shook with sobs. She wrapped her arms around her stomach, as if trying to hold herself together, as the pain of losing Ford ripped her apart.

CHAPTER TWENTY-FOUR

ELIZABETH WOKE THE next morning to the pitter-pattering sound of rain on the window. Disoriented, she rubbed the grit from her dry and aching eyes, blinking to try to get some moisture into them.

Her muscles were sore from sleeping in the cramped space of the window seat all night, and her legs almost buckled as she tried to stand. She took a few seconds to stretch—her body protesting each movement. The attic was chilly, and she wrapped herself in the throw blanket again as she padded downstairs to make coffee.

She wasn't hungry, but she forced herself to eat a few bites of leftover pizza and then washed them down with coffee. But she could barely taste either one.

She let the animals out and stood on the back porch listening to the rain and looking up at the swollen clouds in the sky. The memory of the shooting star she'd seen the night before had her inhaling a deep rain-scented breath as she touched her necklace.

One brave thing at a time. That was how she was

going to get through her day, and then her week, then her month.

She could start with getting herself dressed and unpacking her bathroom. Then she could work on setting up her office.

Don't think about Ford.

It was quite clear from his reaction that he did not love her back. And that he apparently was not interested in a relationship with her, beyond being friends.

So, now she put on her big girl panties and focused on the new life she was trying to make for herself.

Do one thing at a time.

And that started with more coffee and a hot shower.

When Elizabeth came downstairs a few hours later, after showering and unpacking her things into her closet and bathroom, she discovered a steady leak dripping from the ceiling in the mudroom.

Her first instinct when she saw it was to call Ford. But that wasn't an option today. He obviously wanted space. And even though she *really* wanted to text him, especially to thank him for what he had done for her in the attic room, she couldn't bring herself to do it.

She was determined to give him the space he wanted.

So instead of texting him, she took the spaghetti pot she'd unpacked the day before and stuck it under the drip. It's not like she was planning to make pasta today anyway.

Within the next few hours, she'd placed her saucepan and three of her mixing bowls under new leaks and she'd tried, *unsuccessfully*, to put her new desk together.

The instructions were confusing, she couldn't hold up two pieces at the same time to screw them together, and she couldn't find an Allen wrench. In fact, she wasn't certain she even knew what a freaking Allen wrench was. Who was this Allen guy, and what did he do to deserve a wrench being named after him?

The desk and the drips weren't the only problems she'd run into. She couldn't figure out how to work her fancy new oven, and she didn't know where Ford had put the instruction manual. She finally figured out how to preheat the thing, then came running into the room as the smoke alarm beeped and acrid gray smoke poured into the kitchen.

Pulling open the oven door, she discovered the charred remains of the instructions and registration card on the oven rack inside. She jerked back, the smoke stinging her eyes and making her cough as she waved her hands in front of her. She turned it off, then left both the oven and the front door open to clear out the smoke.

It had been drizzly and damp all morning, but the real storms started that afternoon.

Pounding her roof, the rain came down in a deluge as she googled how to order new appliance instructions and what an Allen wrench was while she ate the last piece of lasagna she found in the fridge. She couldn't remember who had brought it by or how long it had been in the fridge, but it still smelled okay, and she only ate half of it anyway.

After what passed for her lunch, she made a cup of hot tea and sipped it as she stared out the window at the mud puddles forming around her car. She thought the rain might have started to let up, then suddenly, as if God had turned on the shower faucet, the rain came pouring down again. Lightning flashed in the sky and thunder rumbled almost immediately after, telling her the lightning strikes were close.

Heavy torrents of water poured from the sky, and she jumped at what sounded like a thousand marbles suddenly hitting her roof.

Thor barked, and Vera stood next to Elizabeth, trembling as she pushed against her legs, as they watched the pea-sized hail fall. It reminded her of popcorn popping in a pan the way the small white balls of ice hit all around the grass then popped back up.

The heavy rain shower lasted almost an hour, then finally let up to a light drizzle again.

The animals had been inside all morning, so this was probably her best chance to let them outside. Elizabeth wiggled her feet into a pair of hot pink flip-flops sitting by the door in the mudroom and followed Thor and Vera outside. Huge puddles filled the backyard too, and the new Adirondack chairs were soaked.

With all the rain, her meandering river was now rushing with muddy water and the debris of fallen trees and branches. It swelled over the banks and the water had risen to where it was halfway up into her backyard.

What would she do if the river completely flooded her yard? Or *her house*? She had no idea how to stop that from happening or how to protect her home. The idea of using sandbags struck her, but she had no idea where to find either the bags or the sand.

Being brave was one thing, but this felt dangerous.

She was going to have to call Ford after all.

Pressing her lips together, she tried not to cry again. She'd tried to change, to make her own choices and step out of her comfort zone, but this all felt like too much. The leaking roof, the flooded yard, the fire she'd almost started in her new kitchen. She couldn't even put a desk together by herself.

Maybe she wasn't courageous after all. Maybe this had all been a big dream that, like her yard, was being washed away in the rain.

Why did she think she could do this? Maybe her parents were right, and she should just flip the house and go back to the city.

A flash of lightning lit the sky, the crack of thunder sounding almost at the same time.

She yelped and called for the animals. But something must have caught Thor's attention, because the little dog took off, barking and running toward the raging water.

"Thor! Stop!" she screamed.

But whatever had captured the interest of the little dog, he had taken after it and there was no calling him back.

Elizabeth ran through the yard, fear gripping her chest as the dog got too close to the water. "Thor! Get back here!"

But her screams were too late.

A wave washed up next to him, and like a watery hand, grabbed the dog and pulled it into the rushing river.

"Thor!" She screamed again and again as she ran toward the river. She lost one sandal in the mud as she sprinted along the shoreline.

She was crying and screaming, terror seizing her heart, as she watched the little orange dog bobbing in the water.

Then she stumbled on a tree root, her feet losing purchase on the slippery bank.

Like the fallen branches, and her sweet dog, the icy water reached for her and pulled her into the raging water too.

CHAPTER TWENTY-FIVE

FORD SLAMMED THE kitchen cabinet shut. He couldn't even remember what he'd been looking for now, but he obviously hadn't found it.

It was well past lunch, and he was hungry and angry, and his mood was fouler than a pissed-off badger cornered by a coyote.

He stared into the next cabinet at the rows of canned soup and chili, but nothing looked good, and he slammed that door shut too.

"Hey now," Duke said, coming in from outside. His cowboy hat was drenched, and water pooled on the hardwood floor as it dripped from his duster. He took both off and hung them on the pegs by the door, then shook his head like a dog coming in from the rain. Pushing his damp shock of hair back over his head, he narrowed his eyes at his grandson. "What's going on with you, Son?"

Ford scowled and growled out the word, "Nothin'."

Duke crossed the room to stand next to Ford. "It's not nothin'. I saw you tear out of here this morning on your horse, galloping across the pasture as if the devil himself were chasing you. Then you were tossing hay bales in the barn like they had personally offended you. And now you're in my kitchen, slamming my cupboard doors."

Ford hung his head. "Sorry."

"I'm not looking for an apology. Though I always appreciate one. But right now, I'm more worried about you. I know you got something stuck in your craw. And I know it's got something to do with your woman. So, spit it out."

Ford stared at his grandfather. "Why do you say that?"

Duke chuckled and clapped a hand on Ford's shoulder. "Because I was married for over sixty years. And I've slammed these cabinet doors a time or two myself."

Ford's shoulders slumped. "Well, Elizabeth isn't *my* woman. Not anymore."

Duke sighed and gestured to the kitchen table. "I'll start us a fresh pot of coffee and make you a sandwich. You better sit down and tell me about it."

Ford slumped down in the chair, his shoulders heavy with the weight of what he'd been carrying all morning. He tried to collect his thoughts, but he still wasn't sure what to say when his grandfather placed a sandwich in front of him then sat down in the chair across from him.

"Eat first," Duke directed.

Ford took a few bites, but the sandwich tasted like cardboard in his mouth. He pushed the plate away. "I don't know what to do."

"I thought things were pretty good between you two. Tell me what happened."

"They *were* good between us. They were great. *She's* great. That's what happened."

"I know I'm an old codger, but I don't get it."

Ford sighed. "Elizabeth is amazing. She's smart and funny and so pretty. Sometimes when I look at her, my heart physically hurts from wanting her so bad."

"Okay. That all seems good. So…?"

"So…that's the problem. She's *too* good. She's too good for a guy like me. She deserves someone better."

Duke raised one bushy eyebrow. "Well, now that's just horse shit."

"It's not. I'm no good for her. She deserves someone who will stick around, who knows what a good relationship is supposed to look like. I don't do relationships. When I'm with a woman and she starts getting too serious, that's my cue to get out."

"Uh, huh. To leave 'em before they leave you?"

He shrugged. "Something like that, I guess."

Duke put his hand over Ford's and gripped it tightly. "Son, I know you've had a time of it. And I know that having both your momma, and that bastard of a father, leave you had to have hurt. Hell, you were just a kid. But instead of always thinking about who walked away from you, try to focus on who stayed. Like your grandmother and me, like your brothers. Those two would do anything for you. And Elizabeth doesn't seem the quitting type to me."

"She told me she loves me."

"That doesn't surprise me a wit. And I know you love her too. But something tells me that's not what you told her."

"No. I told her I had to leave and that we should go back to being just friends."

Duke shook his head. "I think you've been hanging out with that donkey too much, because you're turning into an ass. Now, why would you want to go and say a thing like that?"

Ford scrubbed his hand through his hair. "Because, dammit…I just…ah, hell…I'm ashamed to admit it, but I'm afraid."

Duke tightened his grip on Ford's hand. "Being afraid is nothing to be ashamed of. We all get afraid sometimes. But you can't let fear rule your life. Or dictate *how* you live your life. Otherwise, you might miss out on someone like that sweet gal, Elizabeth. Finding someone to love who loves you back is one of life's greatest gifts. And you can't let fear stop you from accepting that gift."

Ford's voice was barely above a whisper. "But what if she leaves?"

"What if she *stays*?"

Ford's heart twisted with his grandfather's words. He wanted to believe what he was saying. But he'd guarded his heart for so long, never letting anyone get too close. He wasn't sure if he knew *how* to let down his guard and let someone in.

"I've seen the way Elizabeth looks at you," Duke continued. "And the only way that woman is ever gonna leave you is if she *dies*."

"But I've already screwed everything up. I don't know if she'll even talk to me."

"You won't know if you don't try. And she's darn sure not gonna talk to you if you're sitting over here wallowing in your troubles."

"So, what do I do?"

"You go to her. And you tell her you were an idiot for ever letting her go. And that you'll never let her go again."

The icy water stole the breath from Elizabeth's lungs, and she flailed her arms as she tried to keep her head above the water.

The river slammed at her body, splashing water into her face, and trying to drag her under. She swallowed another mouthful of water then sputtered and choked as she tried to get her bearings.

Every few seconds, her head came out of the water enough that she could spot the shore, and she'd try to swim in that direction. But the current had pulled her further out into the river, and she was starting to panic.

She'd lost sight of Thor. Her heart was breaking, but her only focus now was on trying not to drown as the water pulled her under and dragged her further downstream.

Then suddenly, she saw him, caught in a spray of debris up ahead on the side of the bank, his small legs fighting to climb onto a pile of logs and branches around a fallen tree.

With renewed energy, she dug her arms through the water, using every ounce of strength she had to try to swim toward her dog and the fallen tree.

It felt like she was swimming through molasses, the water pushed and pulled at her, but she was making progress toward the pile of debris on the shore.

She reached out her hand. If she could just grab one of the branches.

But just as she got close, a large section of another fallen tree came shooting out of the water and whacked her on the side of the forehead.

Pain exploded in her head, and blackness threatened to close in on her. But she couldn't let herself pass out.

She reached out, one more time, but the water refused to let her go and the ends of the branches slipped through her fingers.

CHAPTER TWENTY-SIX

NOW THAT FORD had decided to go back to Elizabeth, he couldn't get to her fast enough. But the slick and muddy roads had a different idea in mind.

His tires spun and shot clumps of mud as he sped toward her house. A large torrent of water had almost filled the ditch next to the road and threatened to wash out the entrance to her driveway.

He slammed his fist against the steering wheel as his back tire sank into the mud and his truck refused to move forward. As he'd left his ranch, he was overcome with a feeling of fear and dread, and he somehow knew that Elizabeth needed him.

He *had* to get to her.

It wasn't a long drive between their two farms, but he prayed the whole way there that he was worrying for nothing and that she was okay.

He shot up another prayer as he threw the truck in reverse and eased down on the gas. The truck slid to the side, but at least the tire was free. Dixie was in the seat next to him, and she let out a woof as he slammed the truck back into gear and barreled down the driveway.

Splashing through the puddles, he pulled up next to her car, and was practically out the door before he'd even turned the engine off. Dixie jumped down after him, and he slammed the truck door then raced up the porch steps and into the house.

"Elizabeth!" he yelled her name, but he could already feel the house was empty. No little orange dog or mini donkey came racing down the stairs to greet him. He took the stairs two at a time as he raced up to the second level, but those rooms were empty too.

He called her name again as he ran halfway up the attic stairs, then ran back down to the main level after seeing it was empty as well. He went through the kitchen and out the back door of the mudroom, yelling for her one more time.

The river had swelled over the banks and flooded most of her yard. Panic fought the edges of his mind. Had she come out and tried to protect the house from the flooding river? Was she hurt?

Dammit. Why had he been so bull-headed. Why had he left? He would never forgive himself if anything had happened to her.

He froze as he heard a familiar sound and then took off running down the banks of the river. He could see Vera standing by the water, braying, and stamping her feet at the water. She looked like she wanted to go in but was too afraid.

"It's okay, girl," he told the little donkey when he reached her.

Her eyes were wild, and she brayed again, shaking her head at the water as if in a panic.

His eyes caught a flash of color in the mud. His heart stopped as he recognized one of Elizabeth's pink flip-flops sticking out of a long groove of smooth mud that ran into the water. As if she had fallen and been pulled in.

His head whipped back and forth as he looked up and down the raging river. Screaming her name, he sprinted down the bank, his eyes searching for any spot of color, for a hand reaching out of the water, for any sign of her.

Duke's words echoed in his ears. *The only way that woman is ever gonna leave you is if she dies.*

Please God, don't let her die.

A flash of orange caught his eye as he heard the sound of frenzied barking. Bedraggled and shivering, his fur soaking wet, Thor stood on top of a mass of debris and branches next to the bank.

Ford had never been happier to see the little mutt. He scrambled forward, his foot sinking knee deep into the water as he reached for the dog. "Come here, boy," he called. But the dog wouldn't come to him. It just kept barking at the river.

A fist of fear gripped Ford's heart that the dog must have seen Elizabeth in the water.

"Elizabeth!" he screamed again, his throat aching from yelling her name.

He thought he heard his name in reply, but he couldn't see anything in the water, and the sound of it rushing was so loud.

"Elizabeth!"

"I'm here."

He knew he heard something that time. His chest ripped apart, from relief mixed with fear, as he saw a hand barely sticking up from the other side of the debris.

"I'm coming! Hold on!" He grabbed the dog then scrambled back up the bank and put him down next to Dixie. He hadn't even realized the golden had been running behind him. Or that the miniature donkey had been following them too. But both animals stood on the bank.

He raced further down the shore, then tried to carefully climb over the trunk of the fallen tree so as not to dislodge it and send it, and Elizabeth, soaring down the river.

"I see you," he called, spotting her among the branches. "Hold on!"

Her wet hair was matted to her forehead, but instead of its normal chestnut blond color, it shone red with the blood from a cut on the side of her forehead.

He scanned the bank behind him, looking for something he could hold out to her to grab. Spotting nothing, he reached up and grabbed a branch from a tree and tore it loose. Careful not to get pulled into the water too, he reached out the branch. "Elizabeth, grab the branch. I'll pull you in."

She shook her head, just the smallest movement. "I can't. Too tired."

He could see her fatigue and the blue tint of her lips. Her shoulders shook as she shivered in the cold water. He inched closer. Every instinct told him to jump into the water and just grab her. But he couldn't help her if he got sucked down the river too.

Still, he had to do something.

"You can do this," he told her. "You have to. Elizabeth, grab the branch!"

He could see the cut on her head, but he didn't know where else she might be hurt. Or if the wound on her head might have caused a concussion.

He *had* to get her out of the water.

"Please, darlin'. You have to try," he pleaded. "Just reach out your hand and grab the branch."

She nodded her head, just the tiniest of movements, but it was enough to tell him she understood. And that she would try. She lifted one hand from the log she was clinging to and reached for the branch.

"That's it. I've got you. You can do this."

She lifted her other hand and grabbed for the branch.

But it slipped through her fingers.

She let out a small cry as she lost her grip with the other hand, and the water sucked her under and pulled her body away.

CHAPTER TWENTY-SEVEN

FORD DIDN'T THINK. He just dove into the water.

His body seized from the icy shock of it. Then he pushed past the shock, and with three long strokes, he reached her and wrapped his arm around her body.

"I got you." He sputtered out the words as water splashed into his face and mouth.

He was strong, and he'd been swimming in this river since he was a kid. But this wasn't the same river. Flood waters took on a life of their own.

But he couldn't let her die. He wouldn't.

He had a hold of her, and thankfully she wasn't fighting him, which terrified him that she had passed out from the head wound. He knew enough to keep his feet up, and in most instances, he would just let the river take him down until he saw a calmer spot to try to swim to the shore, but he wasn't sure how long she'd been in the water or how bad her injuries were.

He had to get her out of the water.

Using all his strength, he swam diagonally toward the shore, pulling Elizabeth's body with him. He saw another fallen tree sticking out into the water, and he reached out and grabbed a branch. Then he used the tree to help haul them to the bank and up onto the grass.

He collapsed on the shore, dragging in deep breaths as he pulled Elizabeth into his lap. Her arms wrapped around him, clinging to his body, and he held her tightly, trying to contain the violent shakes of her shoulders.

Her eyelids fluttered as she whispered, "Go save Thor."

"I've already got him. He's okay." He pressed a quick hard kiss to her mouth then pulled back to assess the damage of the cut on her forehead. It was still bleeding, but not gushing. "We need to get back to the house." But she didn't have any shoes, and he wasn't sure how she'd maneuver through the cold wet mud.

"I can walk," she whispered. But her legs buckled as she tried to stand.

Ford swept his arm under her leg and lifted her up, cradling her to his body. Instead of following the muddy shoreline, he walked further up into the pasture to get back to the farm. He considered the distance between heading to his ranch or going back to hers, but he gauged hers was probably closer.

All three animals raced along next to him as he hurried through the field and into the house. He sat her gingerly on the sofa then grabbed a throw blanket and wrapped it around her shoulders. He briskly rubbed her arms and legs with the dry blanket.

"I'm o-o-kay," she said between chattering teeth

then held her arms out to Thor. The little dog jumped into her lap, and she pulled him under the blanket and held him to her chest, kissing his furry head. "Thank you for saving him."

"He helped save you," Ford said and gestured to the donkey who had jumped onto the sofa and was crowding against Elizabeth's side. "They both did. Vera was standing at the spot you went into the water and braying her head off at me. And Thor kept barking and wouldn't come to me from the fallen log because he must have known you were clinging to the other side."

"He f-fell in. I was t-trying to save him," she said.

"Come on. We need to get you out of these wet clothes," he told her as he pulled off his cowboy boots, shrugged off his jacket, and peeled off his wet jeans and T-shirt. Wearing only his boxer briefs, he helped her up the stairs and into the master bathroom. He turned on the hot water in the shower then helped her get out of her clothes and under the warm spray.

Stepping in with her, he held her body tightly against him, trying to contain her shivers and give her his body heat. He would give her anything.

He gave them a few minutes in the hot shower and washed the blood from her hair, but he wanted to get her dry and warm and have a chance to take proper care of the cut on her head. And assess if she had any other injuries. He'd already noted a cut on her leg.

He turned off the water and wrapped her in a big towel then dried himself. He should have been cold too, but he figured the adrenaline was still fueling his actions and heating his body.

He wrapped a towel around his waist and gingerly pulled a clean T-shirt over her head. Then he found the first aid kit he'd seen in the bathroom the day before. Now that he could really get a look at it, the cut wasn't as bad as he'd thought. And thankfully, it had stopped bleeding, because the last thing he needed now was to have Elizabeth faint on him from the sight of blood.

Her poor head. The scrape she'd gotten from falling through the porch had mostly healed, and now she had another cut above where that one had been. He applied antibiotic ointment and three steri-strips to her forehead and covered the scratch on her leg with more ointment and a Band-aid.

The two dogs and the donkey were curled together on a blanket in the corner of the bedroom.

"I think the animals have the right idea," Ford said, lifting the edge of the comforter so she could crawl into bed then easing in next to her.

He pulled her to him, wrapping her in his arms and spooning her body into his. "I'm sorry I left. And I'm so sorry I wasn't here."

"You *were* here. You showed up when I needed you the most." She rolled over to face him. "But how did you know I was in trouble?"

He took her hand and pressed it to his cheek. "I didn't. I was coming back to apologize and tell you what an idiot I was and that I never should have walked away from you."

Her eyes widened. "Oh." She pulled her hand back from his and lifted her chin. "Okay, I'm ready."

"Ready for what?"

"For you to tell me what an idiot you were and to say that you never should have walked away from me."

He huffed out a soft laugh. "Elizabeth Cole, I was not just an idiot, but a complete dumbass for walking away from you. I'm more sorry than you will ever know. I knew the minute I walked out the door that I'd made a huge mistake. And all I wanted to do was run back to you."

"Why didn't you?"

"Do I need to repeat that *complete dumbass* thing?" He picked her hand up again, his tone turning serious. "I was afraid. I said the one thing I didn't want to do was hurt you, and that was true. But I was worried about me getting hurt too. I was afraid to trust you."

"I know. And that was my fault. I left you once. But I promise I'll never do that again."

"We've spent so much time talking about you and how you are trying to be brave and do things that scare you, and I am in awe of all the things you've done and accomplished. But now it's my turn to be brave, to do the thing that scares me." He placed a tender kiss on the inside of her palm then pressed her hand to his chest. "I have guarded my heart for so many years, afraid to ever give it away, but I think I gave it to you the first weekend we met. It doesn't make sense. I can't explain how or why it happened so fast, but the simple truth is that I've fallen in love with you."

She leaned forward and pressed a kiss to his hand. "Ever since I met you, I've been attempting to be bold, to take chances, to be fearless. In fact, the first daring thing I'd done in a long time was to take my cousin, Elizabeth's name tag off the table at the rehearsal dinner and leave the one that said 'Bitsy' behind. And somehow, I think I became Elizabeth that day. Not my cousin, but the real me. The woman I've always wanted to be. And that weekend with you, I found myself doing more daring things than I'd ever done." She paused to take in a deep breath, and her voice trembled as she continued. "I'm afraid too, Ford. But you encouraged me to do one brave thing at a time, so now I'm being brave as well. I'm taking a risk and telling you that I've fallen in love with you too. And yeah—it does seem a little crazy—like we barely know each other. But I feel like I've been waiting my whole life for you."

He swallowed at the sudden burn in his throat.

A soft smile curved her beautiful lips. "I think I fell for you the very first time I saw you—running toward me as your dog jumped into my lap."

He grinned. "I think I fell in love with you the moment I saw you crawling out of the bushes after you'd chased after that same silly dog. Or maybe it was when you admitted to eating both of our cupcakes while I was valiantly trying to save your tote bag. Or no, maybe it was when I saw you belly flop into the lake and realized your amazing athletic prowess. Or when you dropped your underwear into the campfire."

She cringed. "Okay, now you're just listing embarrassing things I've done."

He laughed. "But those are all the things that made me fall in love with you. We may have said that we were only pretending to be a couple, but my feelings for you, every time I touched you, kissed you, held you, that was all real. I never had to pretend."

"It was all real for me too."

"Then let's show everyone else it's real too. You're the one I want to stay for. And if you'll have me, I'm never walking away from you again."

CHAPTER TWENTY-EIGHT

A WEEK LATER, ELIZABETH was in the attic room, curled in the window seat and reading a book. Thor and Vera were curled together at her feet. She'd taken the little donkey over to the rehabilitation center to visit Miss Bette that morning. The older woman was getting better but she still had several months before she'd be cleared to go home. And the reunion between her and Vera had brought tears to everyone's eyes.

The door to the attic opened, and Ford came up the stairs with a stack of his Louis L'Amour books in his hand.

"Well, this is the last of it," he said, placing the books on the shelf next to his collection of Farmer's Almanacs. "I'm now officially all moved in."

"Yay." She clapped her hands together then slid her legs over to make room for him on the window seat.

It had taken most of the last week, since they were still finishing the renovations on the house, to get him moved him. But true to his word, since the night of the flood, they hadn't spent a night apart. She'd been a little surprised—and *a lot* excited—

when he'd shown up the next day with a box of toiletries, a suitcase full of clothes, a forty-pound bag of dog food, and Dixie's food and water bowls.

He'd told her that when he'd said that he wanted to show everyone else that they were a real couple, that meant that he was really moving in with her. And she couldn't have been more thrilled.

"I have something for you," he said, pulling a small blue velvet bag from his pocket. "You remember when I gave you that shooting star necklace, and I told you it was because it reminded me of the meteor shower that we watched together?"

"Yes," she said, touching the silver necklace at her neck. "And I haven't taken it off since."

"Well, I didn't tell you the whole story behind that necklace. It wasn't just about the meteor shower. You know that my parents both left me when I was young, but the two people who never left, who showed me what real love was, were my grandparents. And when they were first married, Duke gave my grandmother a star necklace. They had their own story behind it, but it became a symbol of their love." He held the bag out to her. "I talked to Duke about it this morning, and he gave this to me. It belonged to my grandmother, and we both want you to have it."

Elizabeth took the bag. She pulled open the drawstrings and slid a sterling silver necklace with a single diamond-encrusted star pendant into her hand. "It's beautiful. I don't know what to say."

"You don't have to say anything. I appreciate that you've worn that necklace I gave you, but the thing only cost me eighteen dollars, so I wanted you to have something worth a little more. And as much as I love the idea of the shooting star, and the symbolism of reaching for what you want, a shooting star is also a falling star." He pointed to the necklace in her hand. "I wanted you to have a single star, like the North Star, because that star is one that's fixed in the sky. It won't ever fall, and it's been used for thousands of years as a light to guide people home. Whenever I look into the sky, I can always find the North Star. And now my North Star is you. Because you're the light that will always lead me home."

She blinked back tears, but they were happy ones, tears of joy at finding this man, this house, this new life.

Ford Lassiter wasn't just the cute cowboy that she'd fallen in love with at first sight. He was her home too.

Over the last several weeks, she'd faced her fears and found the courage to do so many brave things. She felt stronger too. She had used muscles she didn't know she had, she'd mastered the use of a power drill, and she'd finally figured out what an Allen wrench was. She'd met new people, made new friends, become part of a new family. And she'd taken on the care of a miniature donkey.

And now, she had no doubts, no fear, as she climbed into the cowboy's lap and pressed her lips to his. Apparently, she'd been braver than she thought after all.

The End…
…*and just the beginning*

THANK YOU!

THANKS SO MUCH for reading **Love at First Cowboy**. If you loved this book, it would mean so much if you would please leave a review. And if you want to know what happens with Ford's younger brother, Dodge and the sweet librarian, Maisie, preorder **OVERDUE FOR A COWBOY.**

Be the first to find out when my next books are releasing and hear all the latest news and updates happening by signing up for the Jennie Marts newsletter at: *Jenniemarts.com*

My biggest thanks goes out to my readers! Thank you for loving my stories and my characters. I would love to invite you to join my street team, Jennie's Page Turners!

Also by Jennie Marts

If you want MORE hot cowboys, meet three brothers who are hockey-playing cowboys in the

Cowboys of Creedence series:
Caught Up in a Cowboy
You Had Me at Cowboy
It Started with a Cowboy
Wish Upon a Cowboy

Even more hunky cowboys can be found in the heartwarming (but still steamy)
Creedence Horse Rescue series:
A Cowboy State of Mind
When a Cowboy Loves a Woman
How to Cowboy
Never Enough Cowboy
Every Bit a Cowboy
A Cowboy Country Christmas

If you enjoy small town contemporary romance with cute cowboys-
Try the **Hearts of Montana series:**
Tucked Away
Hidden Away
Stolen Away

If you like hockey romance with cute hockey players and steamy romance-
Try the **Bannister Brothers Books**:
Icing on the Date
Skirting the Ice
Worth the Shot

More small-town romantic comedy can be found in the
Cotton Creek Romance series:
Romancing the Ranger
Hooked On Love
Catching the Cowgirl

If you love mysteries with humor and romance, be sure to check out **The Page Turners Series** where a group of women in a book club search for clues and romance while eating really great desserts.

Another Saturday Night and I Ain't Got No Body
Easy Like Sunday Mourning
Just Another Maniac Monday
Tangled Up In Tuesday
What To Do About Wednesday
A Halloween Hookup: A Holiday Novella
A Cowboy for Christmas: A Holiday Novella

Even more humor-filled mystery fun can be found in my new
Bee Keeping cozy mystery series:
Take the Honey and Run
Kill or Bee Killed

Thanks for reading and loving my books!

~Jennie

ABOUT THE AUTHOR

JENNIE MARTS IS the *USA TODAY* Best-selling author of award-winning books filled with love, laughter, and always a happily ever after. Readers call her books "laugh out loud" funny and the "perfect mix of romance, humor, and steam." Fic Central claimed one of her books was "the most fun I've had reading in years."

She is living her own happily ever after in the mountains of Colorado with her husband, two dogs, and a parakeet who loves to tweet to the oldies. She's addicted to Diet Coke, adores Cheetos, and believes you can't have too many books, shoes, or friends.

Her books range from western romance to cozy mysteries, but they all have the charm and appeal of quirky small-town life. She loves genre-mashups like adding romance to her **Page Turners** cozy mysteries and creating the hockey-playing cowboys in the **Cowboys of Creedence**. The same small-town community comes to life with more animal antics in her latest **Creedence Horse Rescue** series. Her sassy heroines and hunky heroes carry over in her heartwarming, feel good romances from **Hallmark Publishing**. And **Take the Honey and Run** is her newest cozy mystery in the Bee Keeping Mystery series.

Jennie loves to hear from readers. Follow her on Facebook at Jennie Marts Books, Twitter at @*JennieMarts*, and at *jenniemartswriter* on Instagram.

Visit her at *www.jenniemarts.com* and sign up for her newsletter to keep up with the latest news and releases.

Printed in Great Britain
by Amazon